Chogan and the Gray Wolf

Book #1 in the Chogan Native American Series

By

Larry Buege

Gastropod Publishing
Marquette, Michigaan

Larry Buege

No part of this book can be reproduced or transmitted in any form or by any means, electronic or mechanical, including photocopying, recording, or by an information storage and retrieval system without permission in writing from the publisher—except for reviewers who may quote brief passages in a review.

Other books by Larry Buege

Miracle In Cade County (Mystery/Love Story)

Cold Turkey (Political Satire)

Bear Creek (Humorous)

Super Mensa (Techno-Thriller)

Growing Up In Sparta (Autobiography)

William Goodman: Civil War Horsesolder

Native American Series

Chogan and the Gray Wolf

Chogan and the White Feather

Chogan and the Sioux Warrior

Chogan and the Winnebago Merchant

Chogan and the Vision Quest

Published by Gastropod Publishing, Marquette, Michigan
Copyright © 2013 by Larry Buege

Library of Congress Control Number: 2013936763
ISBN: 979-8-9851851-1-9

Ojibway Words

Chogan and the Gray Wolf uses several Ojibway words, which may confuse some readers. Their English translations are listed below. The Ojibway Indians spoke a variation of the Algonquian language, one of the most widely used Native American languages in North America. None of the Indians north of Mexico had a written language; therefore, all spellings are European interpretations and have many variations. Spellings for Chogan's tribe include: Ojibway, Ojibwe, Ojibwa, Ojibubway, Otchipwe, and Chippewa. Americans are more likely to use Chippewa, whereas Canadians prefer Ojibway. Ojibway is an exonym or word used by neighboring tribes and refers to the puckering of Ojibway moccasins. The Ojibway refer to themselves as Anishinabe.

1. Chogan (blackbird)
2. Taregan (crane)
3. Ahanu (he laughs)
4. Opwaagan (pipe)
5. Baggataway (lacrosse)
6. Kanti (sings)
7. Gitche Gumee (Lake Superior)
8. Hassun (stone)
9. Wagosh (fox)
10. Wapatoo (arrowhead, duck potato)
11. Gitche Makwa (Great Bear)
12. Manoomin (wild rice)

Larry Buege

CONTENTS

Chapter   Page

1. The Big Fish - - - - - - - - - - - - - - - - 1
2. The Spring Feast - - - - - - - - - - - - - 5
3. The Climbing Tree - - - - - - - - - - - 14
4. The Hunt - - - - - - - - - - - - - - - - - - 34
5. The Mystery Cave - - - - - - - - - - - 46
6. A Skunk for Ahanu and Taregan - 61
7. Wolf Cubs - - - - - - - - - - - - - - - - - 69
8. Whitefoot - - - - - - - - - - - - - - - - - 80
9. The Hornet's Nest - - - - - - - - - - - 94
10. A Rabbit for Whitefoot - - - - - - -121
11. A Turkey for Mother - - - - - - - - 127
12. A Great Journey - - - - - - - - - - - -138
13. Farewell to Whitefoot - - - - - - - -146
14. The Bear Returns - - - - - - - - - - -158
15. The Rice Harvest - - - - - - - - - - -168
16. The Magic Arrow - - - - - - - - - - -180

Larry Buege

This novel is a multi-media venture that incorporates a series of stand-alone web pages explaining important woodland skills Chogan must master to survive in the hostile wilderness. Make sure you check out these web pages as you find them, but don't cheat and look ahead.

CHAPTER ONE

The Big Fish

It was huge! My hands trembled, and I almost dropped my spear. Trout can't grow that big—but there it was. The fish swam out from behind a submerged boulder and into the current. It nipped at a floating bug, and then returned to the protection of the boulder.

I waited, hoping the fish would swim near the riverbank where I could spear it—no such luck. I would have to wade into the river. The water looked cold, but I would be the envy of my friends if I dragged that monster to the spring feast.

I waited until the fish swam into the current to feed and then I stepped into the water downstream from the boulder. Icy water from the melting snow flowed over the tops of my moccasins and onto my feet.

I approached the boulder with the sun in my eyes, so my shadow wouldn't spook the fish, but when I reached the boulder, the fish was gone. It was still feeding in the current. I placed my spear above the spot where I expected the trout to be when it returned. Then I stood motionless in the water…waiting. Grandfather says fish only see motion. I had to be invisible.

My feet were numb from the icy water. I couldn't wait much longer. Fish could tolerate cold water better than I could. I was about to give up when the dark shadow returned to its spot behind the boulder.

When it was under my spear, I pushed down, pinning the fish to the riverbed. Water splashed around me, drenching my clothes, but I didn't care. I reached down and grabbed my prize by the gills. It took all my strength to lift the fish out of the water and drag it up the riverbank. Even when I lifted its head above my knee, its tail dragged on the ground. No one in our tribe had ever speared such a fish. I would be a hero when I hauled the fish into our village. Tonight they will be singing Chogan's praises around the campfire. Chogan means blackbird in the Ojibway language. But tonight I would be soaring with the eagles. Not bad for a boy of twelve winters.

I was bending down to attach the fish to my stringer when I heard a thrashing noise behind me.

Only one animal makes that much noise walking through the woods. I turned expecting to find a bull moose. Instead, a great bear stood no more than five paces from me. It was larger than any bear I had ever seen. One paw could cover a lily pad, and its claws were longer than Grandfather's fingers. A large mass of muscle rose up between its shoulders. This had to be a powerful animal, and it was glaring at me like a fat coon sizing up a bullfrog it had just cornered. The bear was no doubt hungry. I could tell from the slimy drool dripping down from its open jaws that it considered me the choice selection on today's menu. My first thought was to run, but Grandfather says I should never run from a bear. Bears will chase anyone who runs. Although if I didn't run, the bear already had me! Neither alternative appealed to me. As I considered my options, the beast reared up on its hind legs and gave out such a growl that the woods shuddered with fear. When standing on its hind legs, it was taller than two grown men. The bear was so close its breath swept across my face. It was warm and moist and had a foul odor that reminded me of rotten meat. If I hadn't been so scared, I would have puked on the spot.

    I had no doubt the bear planned to eat me for lunch. Even then, I would be little more than a snack for such a large animal. Perhaps if I offered it something else to eat, it would forget about me. Having no fish to contribute to tonight's spring feast would bring shame to my family, but that was the lesser of the two evils. I lowered my fish to the ground and backed away. The bear walked up to the fish and gave it a sniff with its black nose. I backed farther away. The bear placed a paw over the head of my prize fish and then ripped open the fish's belly with its teeth. I continued walking backwards, until thirty paces separated us. Then I quietly slipped into the woods. I ran as fast as I could toward our village. I'm sure it was my imagination, but I could feel the bear's hot breath against the back of my neck as I ran. It still had the smell of decaying flesh.

CHAPTER TWO

The Spring Feast

Our village sits on the shore of Gitche Gumee, a lake so big it has no far shore. Grandfather says when he was younger he paddled his canoe into the lake for a full day and still couldn't see the other side. Someday I will paddle my canoe for several days and I will find the other side.

Afternoons in our village are normally laid back and quiet, but today everyone was busy preparing for the feast. Several men had returned from a hunt with deer slung over their shoulders, and the women were preparing to cut the meat into strips for drying. There would be no shortage of venison at the feast. I found Grandfather at the center of the village where many logs were stacked for the fire. He was talking to Hassun, the son of my mother's sister. Hassun had seen twenty-one winters; enough to be considered one of the men.

Grandfather turned toward me after he finished his business with Hassun. "Did you spear any fish?" he asked.

"I speared three fish," I replied. "One fish was as big as your thigh and longer than my leg."

"Where is this great fish you speared?" Hassun asked. "I see no fish."

I could tell by his voice he didn't believe me. I wouldn't have believed a fish could grow that big either if I hadn't seen it.

"It was eaten by a bear larger than a cow moose." I spread my arms to show the width of the bear. "It had claws longer than Grandfather's fingers, and when the bear stood on his hind legs, it was as tall as two men."

"Chogan has the imagination of a small child," Hassun said. "I assume this bear also got away?" Hassun gave out a big laugh. "Since you have neither fish nor bear to contribute to the feast, I will drop off a small doe I killed this morning. My arrows flew straight, and I killed two deer. I can spare one to protect the honor of my cousin's wigwam." Hassun walked away chuckling, leaving me alone with Grandfather.

"Grandfather, I really did spear a great fish. There really was a large bear."

"Chogan, your lies bring dishonor to our family. No bear is as tall as two men. Your childish imagination has overcome common sense."

"Yes, Grandfather. Maybe it was only as tall as two short men." I looked down at the ground. I could no longer look Grandfather in the eye. He was right. No bear grows that large. But I knew what I saw. Could my eyes have deceived me?

"Go and help your mother skin the doe Hassun has graciously given us. One that tells such lies must work alongside women."

I was in no hurry to return to our wigwam. I wandered around the village inspecting the food women were preparing for the feast. In addition to meat from deer, beaver, and otter, there would be squash and roasted acorns by the basketful and roots from a variety of plants. It would be great feast. All that would be lacking would be fish—my fish.

"Hey, there's Chogan, the mighty bear hunter," Ahanu said—it hadn't taken long for my morning misadventure to spread throughout the village.

"We have nothing to fear," Taregan added. "We have the mighty Chogan to protect us from bears the size of moose."

They both laughed. Every village has its bully. I had the misfortune of living in a village, which had two of them. Ahanu and Taregan had seen one more winter than I had and considered that justification for making my life miserable. With nothing better to do, they had decided to have some sport at my expense.

Since there was little I could say in my defense, I ignored them and headed toward our wigwam. When I arrived, the doe Hassun had promised to give us was hanging from a tree branch, and Mother was removing the skin with a sharpened stone. Tomorrow she would stretch the hide to dry. My younger sister was tending the fire she would need to dry the meat.

"Hassun said you saw a bear this morning," Mother said. "You must be careful in the woods. There are many dangers for a young boy."

"Yes, Mother." I really didn't want to talk about it, but it was apparently providing quality entertainment throughout the village. Everyone had a comment to express. It would have been better if I hadn't told Hassun and Grandfather.

"Was the bear really as tall as two men?" my sister asked. Kanti had only seen ten winters. She was okay for a little sister except when she wanted to tag along. That was a pain.

"It was a large bear." I left it at that, hoping Kanti wouldn't pursue the topic.

"Some kids are saying you lied about the bear because you couldn't spear any fish." Kanti was not about to let it rest.

"I speared three fish," I replied.

"Chogan, can you cut the meat into strips?" Mother asked.

"Yes, Mother."

I was happy for the diversion even if it was messy. Normally, I hated cutting meat. The bloody meat was sticky, and it drew swarms of flies that circled around like miniature vultures. Still, it was better than discussing the bear. I placed a slab of meat on a flat rock and began cutting it into strips with a sharpened bone. Kanti hung the strips on a rack next to the fire. After several days, the heat would dry the meat into strips that would look like old leather. It wouldn't be as tasty as fresh meat, but it would fill the stomach when fresh meat wasn't available.

Kanti added wet leaves to the fire, creating a cloud of white smoke. That would keep flies away from the meat. Then Mother placed the deer's back leg on a stick and hung it over the fire to absorb the smoky flavor. The roast venison would be our donation to the upcoming feast. It was emitting a mouth-watering aroma by the time I finished cutting the last strip of meat.

"Mother, can I play now?" I could see no further work that needed my attention—not that I looked very hard. Men were competing against a neighboring village in a game of baggataway, and I didn't want to miss the excitement.

"Okay, but take your sister with you."

"Do I have to?"

"She's your sister."

That was not what I wanted to hear. Dragging Kanti around was not my idea of fun. I was too young for the big game, but I had hoped to organize a game with some of the older boys. That would be impossible with my sister in tow. I walked toward the sandy beach.

"Chogan, wait for me."

"Hurry, then. The game's already started." I was tall for my age, and Kanti had to run to keep up with my longer legs.

People from both villages were yelling encouragement to their team. Everyone was so excited with the game, no one mentioned my adventure with the bear. Perhaps that was already old news.

I couldn't see any players, but I assumed they were somewhere on the other side of the crowd. I pushed through the mob of spectators, working my way toward the front with Kanti clinging to my left arm. Finally, we wiggled our way to the front where we could observe the game. Young men wearing nothing more than breech cloths chased each other across the sand. Each man carried a short stick with a wooden loop at the end. Strands of cedar roots woven around the loop formed a basket, which the men used to scoop up the ball made of deer hide. They threw the ball from player to player as they worked their way down field in hopes of scoring a point. There was lots of pushing and shoving. Occasionally, a fight would break out. More than one player left the field with a bloody nose.

"Look, Chogan, Hassun scored a point."

"There will be no living with him now," I said. I liked Hassun, but he was good at every sport. He was a great hunter and could place an arrow through the heart of a deer at fifty paces. Young girls adored him. If a bear tried to steal his fish, Hassun would have chased it away with a hickory switch. I found all that a little too much. I would never admit it, but I wanted to be like Hassun when I grew up.

The young men played well into the afternoon until one of the players scooped up the ball and threw it over the head of his teammate, sending it into the water. Gitche Gumee is icy cold even in the summer, and no one ventured into the water to retrieve the ball. It was just as well. The players were exhausted. The loss of the ball was a welcome excuse to end the game.

"Chogan, I'm hungry." Kanti tugged at my sleeve. I had been hoping she would wander off on her own. That did not appear to be the case. But I was also hungry.

"I'm sure there's more food than even you can eat." For a girl of ten winters, Kanti could pack away the food. It was beyond me how she remained skinny.

As I had expected, food was available in great abundance. Women from each wigwam offered a variety of food for the feast. Kanti and I wandered from one offering to the next like grazing deer.

After everyone had eaten their fill and the sun had sunk into the west, the drums began to beat. The pulsating noise increased as more drummers joined in. It was a simple beat, but the sound of so many drummers filled me with energy, pushing aside the shame of my bear encounter. My feet tapped along with the rhythmic beat. Kanti and I felt compelled to join the dancers circling around the drummers.

It was well after dark when Mother found us. "It's late," she said. "Bedtime."

I couldn't argue the point. My feet ached from hours of dancing, and Kanti was fighting to keep her eyes open. It was a fight she was not capable of winning. But the best part of the festival was yet to come. Men were gathering around the fire to tell their stories.

"Mother, can I stay a little longer? I'll be with Grandfather." Grandfather had moved into our wigwam after my father died of the fever. I was much younger then, and all I remember of Father is that he was tall and powerful. Grandfather says he was a great hunter.

"You can stay a little longer, but remember you have to check your snares in the morning."

Kanti offered no similar appeal. She was ready for bed.

Without Kanti tugging on my elbow, I was free to go as I pleased. Where I was going now was not a place for girls—or women. Actually, it wasn't a place for boys either, but if I were quiet, no one would notice. I crept toward the fire but stopped while still in the shadows. I have good ears, and the men were boisterous. They were easy to hear.

The tribal elders were first to speak, and Grandfather stood to give his account. I knew what he would say; I had heard his tale many times. Still, I found it enjoyable. He told of his youth when he traveled west for many moons. He arrived at a land with no trees, only grass. He told of big, shaggy deer that covered the land as far as one could see. Their shoulders and chests were thick like a moose, but they had short necks. I found all that hard to believe, although the men in the circle nodded in agreement. Grandfather was well respected in the village. No one dared call him a liar.

What I liked best was when Grandfather described the hills. He said they were purple and so tall they rose up to kiss the sky. He said at the tops of the hills it was winter all year long, and snow covered their peaks. Someday I will travel west to see those hills.

Several other village elders rose to speak. They told of terrible winters past and how they hunted on snowshoes to save the village from famine. Finally, Hassun rose to speak. I wondered what he would say. He was young and not yet in possession of many great adventures. I heard him mention my name. He was telling of my encounter with the bear, but now the bear was the height of three men, and the claws were longer than a man's forearm. People around the fire were laughing. They were laughing at me. Maybe the bear wasn't as tall as two men, but it was big. I crept back to the wigwam with tears in my eyes.

***
Baggataway

Historians have variously described the Native American game of baggataway as a religious experience, a method for training warriors, or merely a sport played for fun. Whatever the case may be, there is little doubt baggataway is the oldest sport ever played on the American continent. Rules varied from tribe to tribe, but in most cases the object was to send a stuffed deerskin ball through the goal at the far end of the field.

Players caught and advanced the ball using hooked sticks similar to a shepherd's staff. A mesh of leather straps attached to the hook provided a pouch for catching the ball. The first Europeans to observe this game were Jesuit missionaries who named it lacrosse after the staff or *crosier* held by Jesuit Bishops. Modern lacrosse has formal rules and is played at many of the larger universities.

The most famous baggataway game occurred at Fort Michilimackinac on June 2, 1763 during Pontiac's Rebellion. Unarmed Ojibway warriors began the game in front of the fort's main gate. When the British soldiers came outside to watch, the warriors commenced their attack. Ojibway women standing near the gate produced weapons from under their clothing and handed the weapons to the warriors as they rushed into the fort. The Ojibway took possession of the fort within minutes.

Please check out the below web site
the-gray-wolf.com/baggataway/
***

CHAPTER THREE

The Climbing Tree

When I awoke, the wigwam was empty. Kanti and Mother were outside fixing breakfast from the previous night's leftovers. As usual, I was the last to awaken. I sat up on my sleeping bench and rubbed my eyes awake. Neatly folded fur blankets lay at the ends of the other sleeping benches lining the inside wall of our wigwam. My sleeping bench was never that tidy. The benches elevated us from the ground, so the earth would not suck away our warmth. It was spring when the days were warm, but the nights remained chilly. Grandfather must have started a fire before he left. The soft flames in the fire pit at the center of the wigwam took the chill out of the air. Crawling out of the blankets into cold air would have been unbearable. The smoke from the fire curled upward and exited through the hole at the top of the wigwam, although a smoky smell still clung to the walls and blankets.

"It's about time you woke up." Mother filled a wooden bowl with the leftovers and passed the bowl to Kanti. Kanti was much too cheerful when she brought the bowl to me.

"Mother says I may go with you when you check your snares."

I was about to offer a protest when Mother gave me a stern look. I had seen that look before. She had made a decision, which no argument on my part would alter. "Kanti is old enough to help," she said. That was the end of the argument.

The food wasn't as tasty as it had been the night before, but it still made my mouth water. Mother had mixed pieces of meat with roasted vegetables and ground acorns. The meat tasted like beaver, but I couldn't be sure.

"I could be gone all day," I said. It was a feeble protest, but I felt the need to make my position known, even if Mother ignored it.

"We have dried venison you can take for lunch. You won't go hungry."

I ate the rest of my breakfast in silence. I enjoyed checking my snares. The forest was my home. When I walked quietly, I could hear the woods. It spoke to me, like a well-placed whisper. At other times the woods overflowed with music and joy that seemed to come from nowhere and everywhere all at the same time. Now all I would hear would be Kanti's endless chatter. So would the woods, and the music would cease in protest.

"I'll pack our pouches with dried meat." Kanti was bubbling over with enthusiasm—enthusiasm I did not share. Mother made deerskin pouches for us several years ago. They were just big enough to hold a few essentials. The attached leather straps allowed us to drape the bags over our shoulders. Kanti placed four large pieces of venison in each bag. That was more than I would normally eat; Kanti's stomach was more demanding than mine.

"I rubbed grease on my moccasins in case the ground is damp." Kanti lifted up a foot to show off her moccasins; it would be a long day.

I handed the empty bowl to my mother and picked up my spear. Kanti watched with anticipation. "You can carry the club," I said. I gave her my club, which she accepted as if it were a prized possession. If she was coming along, she might as well share the work. Perhaps next time she would not be so anxious.

"Why do we need a club?" The club was nothing more than an oval-shaped rock polished over the years by the waves along the shore of Gitche Gumee. I had attached it to the wooden handle with leather thongs.

"If we catch an animal in one of the traps, we'll have to kill it. Otherwise the animal will be complaining all the way back to the village." The sarcasm was lost on Kanti, but not on my mother.

She gave me a cold stare, a subtle reminder that I was pushing my luck.

"Make sure you drink plenty of water," I told Kanti. "The day will be hot, and we won't have access to good water until late in the morning." I drank my fill from an earthen jar and passed the water jug to Kanti who did likewise.

"You ready?" I asked. Kanti just smiled at me. The stone club looked out of place in her small hands.

I headed down a trail, which led south from our village. Kanti half walked and half ran trying to keep up with my longer legs.

"Doesn't this trail take us to that other great lake?" she asked.

"Only if you want to walk for two days."

"Where are your traps?"

"In the woods. We'll be in the woods soon enough."

"But we are in the woods."

"No, we're on a trail. The woods are on either side of us."

"How long do we stay on the trail?"

"Not long."

"Won't we get lost?"

"Not if you stay with me. See that bend in the trail. That's where we head into the woods." I had been hoping for a little peace and quiet, but Kanti's chatter continued without pause. She had a never-ending stream of questions.

The trail connecting the two lakes with no distant shore was well worn. I had never been to the other lake, but many travelers made the journey each year, trampling the vegetation down to bare earth. No one could lose his way on such a well-marked trail. Once we left the path, there would be no markings to guide our way. Only individuals who were one with the woods dared venture from the trail.

We turned right at the bend in the trail and headed into the forest. Since it was early spring, the undergrowth was minimal. Later in the year, walking through the woods would be more difficult.

"Where are your snares?"

"The first one is about six hundred paces from the trail."

We soon arrived at a section of the river where a fallen tree offered a dry path across most of the river. Two large boulders provided steppingstones for the rest of the way.

"Follow me," I said. I grabbed a branch from the fallen tree to provide stability and started across.

"We were lucky to find a spot where we can cross the river without getting wet."

"That wasn't luck."

Kanti is naturally agile and walked across the log without the assistance of any branches. She made the crossing look easy.

My first two snares were empty. That was not unusual. Trapping small animals wasn't an easy task. At the third snare we found a rabbit swinging from a leather thong attached to a tall sapling. The sapling bowed under the animal's weight. When it saw us coming, the rabbit began wiggling. I grabbed it by the hind legs.

"Hit it on the head with the club."

Kanti scrunched up her nose. "You hit him."

I gave the rabbit a thump on the head with Kanti's club and it lay still. "Here, do you think you can at least carry the rabbit?" I passed the dead animal to Kanti. Then I pulled down on the cord to reset the snare. After I bent the sapling almost to the ground, I attached the cord to a stick, which I then wedged under a log. Another cord, also attached to the sapling, had a loop with a slipknot at its end. I placed this loop in the gap between two large boulders, keeping the loop open with small twigs. Any animal walking through the gap would catch its head in the loop and pull the wedged stick from under the log. If everything worked as planned, the sapling would yank the animal into the air where it would patiently await my next visit.

The next twelve snares were unproductive, although two snares had been sprung and needed to be reset. It took many snares to provide a consistent source of fresh meat.

Traps and Snares

Trapping was far more efficient than hunting. Chogan's traps worked twenty-four hours a day and didn't require his presence, which could scare away game. His traps fell into one of three categories.

Chogan created simple snares by hanging a loop from an overhead branch. He used small twigs to hold the loop open. When a duck or grouse walked into his snare, the loop wrapped around the bird's neck and tightened as the bird struggled. Chogan set his snares along well known animal trails where he was more likely to catch something, although he sometimes lured animals into his snares with bait. Sometimes, he placed obstacles on both sides of the loop to herd animals toward the snare.

Spring-pole snares worked best for rabbits, snowshoe hares, and other animals capable of chewing the cord and escaping. Chogan made his spring-pole snares by tying a noose to the end of bent-over sapling. He used a variety of trigger mechanisms to hold the sapling in place, relieving the loop from the sapling's tension. When the rabbit or other small animal tripped the snare, the sapling sprang upward, lifting the animal into the air where it was difficult for the animal to chew its way free.

The deadfall was the most difficult trap for Chogan to make and required all of his strength. It looked like a simple lean-to shelter except it was constructed from heavy logs. When an animal tripped the deadfall, the logs crashed down on the animal, killing it. Sometime Chogan used smaller logs and then placed heavy rocks on top to add weight. A crib-like structure, made of vertical poles embedded in the ground, prevented the animal from jumping clear of the falling log. Chogan used deadfalls mostly for beaver and other larger animals. If you wish to read more about how Chogan made his snares, check out http://www.the-gray-wolf.com/snares.html on your computer.

Please see **the-gray-wolf.com/snares/**

"Fifteen snares and all we got is one rabbit. That isn't much to show for the work we've done." Kanti had the rabbit's hind legs tied to the strap of her leather bag, and the rabbit now slapped against her thigh with each step. She carried the club draped over her right shoulder like a seasoned warrior, making her look pretty tough for a girl of ten winters.

"You didn't have to come," I reminded her.

"Someone has to carry your rabbit."

"The next snare should be more productive. I placed it on a beaver run with lots of tracks. Wait until you tie a large beaver to your strap. It'll make that rabbit feel like a puny ground squirrel."

I was filled with optimism when I saw the trap; it had been sprung. Beaver were too big for whip snares. Instead, I used a log-fall. When the beaver dislodged the trip stick, one end of a heavy log would fall on its head, crushing him. Even from a distance, I could see that the log had fallen.

"What happened to the beaver?" Kanti asked once we got close. All that remained of the beaver were the tail and a disfigured head. A few smelly pieces, which I assumed were intestines, clung to the log. I bent down to study the tracks left in the mud. Most of them were beaver tracks, but mixed in with them were wolf tracks.

"Wolf," I said.

"A wolf pack?" It takes a lot to scare Kanti, but I could see she was nervous.

"Probably a loner. If a pack were involved, they would have eaten everything, even the head and tail. This was done by a lone wolf that ate its fill and left."

"Will it come back?"

"Wolves fear people. They won't bother us. You'll be lucky if you ever see one. I've only seen wolves twice—both times from a distance."

There was no sense resetting the trap. No beaver would come close to the trap now. "The next set of snares is at the north end of Wagosh Lake," I said. It was a good hike from our current location. I headed east with Kanti one pace behind.

"How are we going to find Wagosh Lake?" she asked. "The woods all looks the same."

"We follow a straight line in that direction," I told her, pointing toward where the lake should be.

"But if we walk in a straight line we'll run into trees and large boulders. We'll have to walk around them."

"That won't be a problem as long as you don't walk around the same side each time. Otherwise you'll walk in a circle. If you go to the left the first time, the next time you must go to the right."

Kanti was quiet for moment while she pondered the consequences of consistently going around an obstacle in the same direction. I slowed my pace, so she could walk beside me. I would have to teach her the ways of the woods like Grandfather had taught me.

"Yuck, what is that smell."

At first I didn't know what Kanti was talking about; then the nauseating odor hit me. Something was very dead, and it wasn't a small animal. Curiosity got the best of me, and I headed toward the foul smell. I always wanted to know what was happening in the woods. We had walked no more than thirty paces when we came upon a cow moose lying on its side. Foul gas bloated and deformed its stomach. I assumed the moose had been dead for two days. Some animal had eaten a good portion of the rump. A swarm of flies labored over what remained. It never takes flies long to find the dead. The head of the moose was partially severed at the neck. I looked around searching for clues that might explain what had happened. On some of the lower branches, I found leaves speckled with dried blood. The moose had died a violent death. But that was not what caught my attention. Looking up at a white birch tree not far from the moose, I discovered scratch marks that were too high on the tree for even a tall man to reach.

"Did wolves do this?" Kanti asked.

"No," I said.

Kanti looked at me, waiting for additional information. She was never satisfied with a yes or no answer. She insisted on explanations.

"A wolf pack can bring down a moose, but they attack the legs, biting into the tendons until the moose falls. See the blood on the leaves. The neck arteries were cut while the moose was still standing."

There was considerable meat remaining on the moose. Whatever killed the moose might return. My small spear would be of little use if it did. "Kanti, we need to leave...now!"

I began running toward my next set of snares. I looked behind me to see if Kanti was keeping up, but she ran effortlessly like a deer. She didn't even appear winded. The dead rabbit slammed against her thigh with each stride.

I slowed down when we approached Wagosh Lake where I had hidden my remaining four snares. We were far enough from the moose that I no longer felt any danger.

One of the four snares provided a medium-sized raccoon. I quickly dispatched it with the club. The rabbit and raccoon would provide sufficient meat for supper, although I still regretted losing the beaver. I preferred beaver meat over rabbit or raccoon.

"Chogan, can we eat now? I'm hungry."

I was surprised Kanti, with her bottomless pit, hadn't asked earlier. "I suppose we can eat. There's an open area down by the lake where we can eat in the sun. If I remember right, there's even a log we can sit on."

My memory hadn't failed me. A fallen birch tree lay on a grassy area ten paces from the lakeshore. The tree had fallen during a recent winter storm and had not yet begun to rot. Deer or moose had visited the area searching for food and had chewed the grass short. It provided a good spot to eat our lunch.

"Look, Chogan, there's some *wapatoo*." Kanti pointed to a patch of aquatic plants with large arrow-shaped leaves protruding above the water along the shore. "We can have *wapatoo* with our dried meat."

"It's only spring. That water has to be cold." I was hoping she wasn't serious. With Kanti, you could never tell.

"But the day is hot. The water will cool us off." Kanti was already removing her moccasins—she was serious.

Kanti waded into the water, where her feet quickly sank into the muck. The lower edge of her leather skirt grew dark as it became wet. But Kanti was right; it was a warm day. Her skirt would quickly dry.

"Chogan, come and help. The water isn't that cold."

"Even if you find some *wapatoo*, they'll taste bitter unless we cook them."

"Then cook them. We can roast them over a fire."

"We don't have a fire."

Kanti placed both hands on her hips and stood in knee-deep water, giving me that exacerbated look. She could say a lot without words—not that she was often silent.

"Okay, if you can find some *wapatoo*, I'll build a fire."

Roasted *wapatoo* was hardly worth the effort, but I took off my moccasins and waded into the water to join Kanti. She was right: With the day being so hot, the cold water on my legs felt refreshing. Still, I would have been satisfied with the dried venison.

My feet sank into the muck. It was a strange sensation. I moved my foot around until I found a *wapatoo* tuber. Once I loosened it from the mud, it floated to the surface. Kanti already had several stored in a pouch she had created from the front of her skirt. Mother would be pleased if we brought some *wapatoo* home along with the rabbit and raccoon.

Not having a skirt to store the *wapatoo* tubers, I tied mine together using their attached roots. It didn't take long before I had over twenty tied in a bunch. They were quite plentiful. Fall is the best time to harvest *wapatoo*, but early spring, when they have been dormant over the winter, isn't a bad time either.

Wapatoo

Wapatoo or arrowhead is a prolific aquatic plant found along the shorelines of freshwater lakes and slow-moving streams throughout the United States and Canada. The plant received its English name from the arrowhead-shaped leaves protruding above the water. Each leaf rests on top of a one-half to three-foot stalk. During August and September, picturesque three-petaled, white flowers bloom in coils near the tops of their individual stalks.

The above ground portion of the plant did not interest Chogan and Kanti. They wanted the tubers attached to the roots buried deep in the mud. The tubers are similar to potatoes in taste and texture although smaller, ranging from pea-size up to the size of a hen's egg. The nutritious tubers can be eaten cooked or raw, although raw tubers have a mildly bitter taste. Roasting, boiling, or baking removes any bitter taste.

Americans Indians like Chogan and Kanti harvested the tubers in early spring or late fall by wading barefoot among the plants. They used their toes to loosen the tubers from the mud. Once freed from the mud, the tubers floated to the surface where they were gathered. Ojibway Indians stored tubers for winter by boiling them and then slicing the tubers and hanging them to dry.

European settlers learned about the plant from Native Americans and used the tubers extensively until their regular crops became available. The arrowhead tubers were a mainstay for members of the Lewis and Clark expedition.

Please see **The-gray-wolf.com/wapatoo/**

Some people eat the tubers raw, but I find the taste unpleasant. I prefer them roasted, which meant I needed a fire. I found some cattails along the shore. Their flowering stalks from last fall were dead and dry. Fluffy fibers covered the top of the cattails. I could use them for tinder. I selected a dry cattail shoot for my spindle, making sure the shaft was straight. For the hearth board, I used a branch from a dead basswood tree. I split the branch in half using a sharp rock for a wedge, which I hit with my stone club. Then I filed a notch in the edge of the wood using a rough stone.

"You sure you need *wapatoo* with your dried venison?" Lunch was turning into a major project. It would have been much simpler if I had come alone.

"I'll help you start the fire." Kanti knelt on the ground facing me with the spindle and hearth board between us.

I placed my foot on the hearth board to hold it fast and then began spinning the spindle between my palms. I pressed down on the spindle as it spun and my hands slowly moved downward toward the hearth board. As my hands approached the bottom, Kanti began spinning from the top of the spindle. Her hands also worked their way downward. The spindle continued to spin without pause as we alternated our hands. Soon black powder filled the notch and smoke curled upward. I blew on the smoking powder and it glowed red.

"Nothing to it," Kanti said. I had to admit, with both of us alternating on the spindle, it did work quite quickly. It would have taken much longer if I had worked by myself. I added dry grass and some bark from a dead log, while Kanti prepared roasting sticks.

"Here, Chogan." Kanti gave me a stick with three walnut sized *wapatoo* tubers skewered on its end. She had four on her stick.

"Thank you," I replied. Now that we had done the work, I was looking forward to eating roasted *wapatoo* with my venison. Dried meat by itself gets old quickly. We ate in silence. I didn't know what Kanti was thinking, but I couldn't push the dead moose from my mind. Grandfather says some animals must die so others can live. I understood that. That is the way of the woods, but there was something unnatural about the way the moose had died.

"Chogan, do we have any more snares to check?" Kanti asked after she had finished eating.

"We just checked the last one. We can go home now."

"I'm going to climb that tree."

Without waiting for a reply, Kanti ran toward a lone spruce at the lake's edge. The trunk of the tree was almost two of my paces in diameter. The giant spruce towered majestically over the lake as if it were the lake's guardian. Large branches protruded out along the entire length of the trunk, creating the perfect climbing tree.

"Chogan, come on up," Kanti said from her perch on one of the lower limbs. Then she continued her way upward.

It had been years since I had climbed a tree for the sheer enjoyment of climbing. I had to admit I had never seen such a good climbing tree. I laid my spear against the birch log and began climbing. I was not as fast as Kanti. No one was as fast as Kanti. She sprang from branch to branch with the grace and agility of a red squirrel. I would never admit it, but Kanti was a better athlete than I. She climbed until the branches were too small to safely support her weight and then waited for me to catch up.

"Chogan, you can see forever from up here…Look there's Gitche Gumee."

Through the branches I could see a long line where water reached up to touch the sky. Even from this height, I could see no distant shore. I sat beside Kanti and admired the view. I had passed this way many times but never considered climbing the tree.

"Chogan, this is more fun than staying with Mother. Thank you for taking me with you."

I was about to remind her it wasn't my idea, but thought better of it. It had been a pleasant day. And the *wapatoo* had tasted good—despite the extra work. Except for Kanti's endless chatter, she had been a good companion.

"Chogan," Kanti whispered. She tugged at my sleeve and pointed to the edge of the lake. I saw nothing to warrant a whisper. Then I saw it. No farther than fifty paces from our tree, a dark-shaped phantom drifted effortlessly among the shrubs. The animal sniffed the air and then looked both ways before walking down to the lake for a drink.

"Chogan, it's a wolf, a real wolf."

This was the third time in my life I had seen a wolf—although never before at such a close distance. Wolves are wary animals, but they never expect danger from above. We must have been downwind or she would have smelled the fire as well as us. Most people reserved the highest respect for the black bear. For me, it is the gray wolf. They are the masters of the woods.

"Kanti, see her swollen belly. She will soon have a litter." I strained to find other wolves, but she was alone. For some reason, wolves had expelled her from the pack. "If she's the wolf who ate my beaver, she is welcome to it. She'll need the extra fat when she begins nursing her pups."

We continued watching in silence. Several times the wolf looked our way, but never up. Finally, she quenched her thirst and disappeared into the woods as mystically as she had arrived.

"She is a beautiful animal," Kanti said after a few moments of rare silence. "I hope she has many babies."

I continued to sit in silence. I was sure Kanti knew I was in full agreement. The woods held no finer animal.

After a few more moments of silence Kanti said, "It was the bear, wasn't it?"

"What was the bear?"

"That killed the moose."

"Bears can't bring down a moose," I said.

"Not an ordinary bear. A bear that can stand as tall as two men could bring down a moose. Chogan, I saw the scratch marks on the tree. If I stood on your shoulders, I still couldn't touch those marks. It had to be same bear that stole your fish. If he comes after us, I'll hit him in the nose with my club." Kanti pulled the club out from under her belt and gave it a few swings.

"If it were the same bear I saw, you wouldn't be able to reach his nose. You'd have to hit him in the knee. Besides, you can't even hit a rabbit."

"For a bear that large, I'll make an exception."

I waited until Kanti had returned the club to its place under her belt. "Kanti, it is best if you don't tell Grandfather what you think. The moose was killed by a pack of wolves."

"What about the blood on the tree leaves and the bear markings on the tree? It had to be a bear."

"Trust me. No one will believe you. Bears can't bring down moose. Come, it's time we headed back."

CHAPTER FOUR

The Hunt

I awoke early thinking the day was mine to do as I pleased. I checked my snares every other day. Any animal caught today would still be there tomorrow, and that was fine with me. I had discovered a cave along the shore of Gitche Gumee that I needed to explore. It wasn't a big cave, but it appeared to have several interesting passageways I could investigate.

I wasn't surprised to find everyone already up and productive. Mother and Kanti were weaving mats from cattail reeds. Enough reeds lay at their feet to keep them occupied most of the day. Mother wanted to cover the floor with cattail mats to keep out the mud on rainy days. I was glad Mother didn't expect boys to weave mats. It looked boring.

"Mother, where's Grandfather?" As usual, Grandfather had left before I awoke. I wanted to discuss the cave with him. There wasn't much he didn't know. I was sure he had explored the cave at some time in his past.

"He's going hunting with the men. If you hurry you can catch him before he leaves."

Getting near enough to shoot deer with an arrow required considerable luck as well as skill. It was much easier if hunters chased the deer into a narrowed area where the best archers were waiting. Grandfather says most tasks are easier when people work together.

I found Grandfather near the medicine lodge. He was discussing the hunt with several tribal elders. The younger men performed the hard work, but the tribal elders still planned the hunt.

I waited at a polite distance until Grandfather and the other elders nodded in unison. I assumed they had reached an agreement. The elders then dispersed to inform the others. Grandfather glanced in my direction with a look of surprise. He had been unaware of my presence.

"Chogan, aren't you checking your snares today?"

"No, Grandfather, not today. I checked them yesterday. I caught a rabbit and a raccoon. I'll check them again tomorrow."

Grandfather looked me over, paying particular attention to the spear I held in my right hand. "Are you interested in using that spear?" he asked.

I was hoping Grandfather wasn't suggesting another fish-spearing adventure. The encounter with the bear was still fresh in my memory. I had no desire to repeat the experience.

"Yes, Grandfather. I suppose I am. What do you wish me to spear?" I knew he would suggest trout. Trout was his favorite fish. I tried to think of a valid excuse for declining Grandfather's request, but nothing came to mind.

"Today we will be hunting deer near Wagosh Lake. I believe you have some snares there."

"Yes, Grandfather. I have four snares on the north end of the lake."

"Are you familiar with that outcrop of rock that rises up three times the height of a man near the east shore?"

"Yes, Grandfather. I've been there many times."

"It's about forty paces from the lake. This afternoon we'll be chasing deer into that narrow area between the lake and the rocks. Our best archers will be hiding behind the rocks waiting for them. We should shoot many deer today."

"Yes, Grandfather." I was wondering why Grandfather was explaining the plan in such detail. He had never done so in the past unless I specifically asked.

"Chogan, you have seen twelve winters and are old enough to participate in the hunt. Would you like to join us?"

I couldn't believe what I was hearing. Deer hunting was a man's activity. Grandfather was asking me to join the men. I immediately lost interest in the cave. I could explore the cave another day.

"Yes, Grandfather. I would be honored to join you on the hunt."

"We will be gone most of the day. Make sure you tell your mother."

***

We began the hunt on the north side of Wagosh Lake. Sometimes—when there was a gap in the treetops—I could see our climbing tree in the distance. The spruce towered above the other trees in the woods making it a good reference point, not that I needed one. It was hard to get lost in the woods with Grandfather at my side. He spread us out in a long line facing the lake. Grandfather was fifty paces to my right and another man patiently waited an equal distance to my left.

"Everyone ready?" Grandfather asked. He looked around, checking to ensure all the hunters were in the proper position. The hunters raised their bows or spears to signal they were ready. I did likewise. It made me feel like one of the men. "Let's go," Grandfather said after counting the raised weapons. Grandfather says it is important that everyone maintains the proper position during a hunt or the deer would sneak through the lines.

We began walking toward the lake. Some men were singing; others were whistling or just shuffling their feet in the leaves. Noise was important. It was a strange experience for someone taught to walk silently. I carried my spear, but I wouldn't need it today. The true hunters were hiding in the rocks on the east side of the lake. I was sure Hassun would be one of them. Someday I, too, would be a great hunter.

Most of the time I could see Grandfather as well as the man on my left, but sometimes they would disappear in the brush. I continued walking at the same pace until they reappeared. The hunt was not as exciting as I had hoped. I did see one deer in the distance, but that was all. Except for the noise we made, the woods was quiet. We walked slowly. Grandfather wanted us to guide the deer, not cause a stampede. No one can hit a running deer with an arrow, not even Hassun.

As we approached the lake, I saw a gray shadow moving through the brush ahead of me. It was only fleeting glimpses. I thought it must be a deer at first, until the animal stepped into a clearing and looked back at me. It was the she-wolf. She just stared at me for a moment and then disappeared into the woods. I think I was the only one who saw her. She was caught in the same trap as the deer. Given a choice, wolves prefer to run from man. But while trying to escape our marching line of men, she would follow the deer into a shower of arrows. We don't normally hunt wolves for food, but wolves still provide edible meat, and they compete with us for deer. If she entered the kill zone, I knew they would shoot her.

My joy of the hunt quickly turned to sadness. She was a beautiful animal. I didn't want her to die. And she was about to have pups. That alone should be reason to spare her life. I was hoping she might slip through our lines, but the space between the hunters narrowed as we approached the lake. There was no way she could escape.

Grandfather motioned for us to slow down when we reached the north side of Wagosh Lake. He said the deer should be wandering into the gap between the rocky outcrop and the lake. He didn't want to spook them. I mentally visualized Hassun shooting the deer as they walked through the narrow passageway. Then I visualized him shooting the she-wolf as she followed the deer into the danger zone. I wanted to shout. I wanted to warn the wolf. But it wouldn't have done any good. The wolf had seen me, and she could hear us coming through the woods. The wolf would be too far ahead of us by now. Any shouting would only hasten her approach toward the trap.

It seemed like forever before we arrived at the end of our hunt. Hassun and four other hunters were standing in the clearing, holding their bows high in celebration. They shot six deer—far more than anyone had expected. They laid the six deer side by side on the ground for everyone to see. Everyone was jubilant except me. I nervously looked around expecting to see my beautiful wolf hanging from a tree branch by her feet, or lying on the ground in a pool of blood. I was relieved to find no sign of the wolf. Somehow she had escaped. Once I knew my wolf was safe, I joined the celebration. My first hunt had been a great success. Some of the men even let me help carry the deer back to camp.

I was walking tall when I returned to our village and leaned my spear against our wigwam. Mother and Kanti were still weaving reed mats. They almost had enough mats to cover the floor of our wigwam. Weaving mats was an important job, but it couldn't compare with bringing six deer back from a hunt.

"Hi, Mother," I said. "We got six deer." I tried to sound casual, as if it were something I did routinely.

"That's great," Kanti said. Mother just smiled, but I knew she was proud of her son.

"Chogan did the work of a man today," Grandfather said.

I hadn't been aware of his presence behind me. Sometimes Grandfather walks with the silence of a butterfly—totally non-existent until it lands on your shoulder and spreads its wings to let you know it's there. Grandfather was holding his beautifully crafted bow and a quiver filled with three arrows.

"Chogan, someday you will do more than chase the deer. You must learn to hunt the deer, but to do that you will need a good bow." Grandfather passed his bow to me. It was the same bow he carried with him when he followed the sunset to the land with no trees. It was the same bow that shot the shaggy deer with the thick shoulders like a moose. That bow was his life. He was never without it.

"Grandfather, I can't take your bow."

"Chogan, I am getting too old for the hunt. Whom else should I give it to? Your father was a great hunter. Perhaps if you practice with this bow, you can be as good as he was. Someday your arrows could fly truer than those of Hassun—but only if you practice."

I reluctantly accepted the bow. It was difficult to think of Grandfather being too old for the hunt. Grandfather had handcrafted the bow out of hickory. Years of use had rubbed the wood smooth. A piece of hide from the shaggy deer covered the grip. It was a beautiful bow. I would be the envy of the village boys.

"Grandfather, I don't know how to thank you."

"Use it wisely, Chogan. Use it wisely. That will be plenty of thanks. I'm sorry I only have three arrows. Tonight after we eat, I will show you how to shoot the bow. I'll also need to teach you how to make straight arrows. The bow is useless when shooting crooked arrows."

I had made arrows in the past for Hassun, but they looked nothing like the beautiful arrows in Grandfather's quiver.

That evening Grandfather showed me how to shoot the bow. It's not as if I had never shot a bow, but try as I might, I couldn't shoot my arrows as straight as Grandfather. His arrows always hit the target. I would practice. Someday my arrows would fly as true as Hassun's arrows and perhaps even Grandfather's arrows. Grandfather showed me how to bind feathers to the arrow's shaft and how to find the best stones for the arrowhead. I would make many arrows to fill my quiver.

I practiced late into the evening—even after Grandfather left—and then I woke up early to practice some more. It was the day I was to check my snares, so I couldn't practice as much as I wanted. I would practice again when I returned from checking my snares.

Kanti had packed our pouches with food. She assumed she would be helping me check the snares. I didn't argue the point. I wanted to check them quickly and could use the extra help. I placed the quiver with its three arrows over my shoulder and grabbed my bow.

"Aren't you taking your spear?" Kanti asked.

"No, I have Grandfather's bow now." I headed down the trail.

Kanti grabbed my spear and followed me. The spear meant a lot to me. With Grandfather's help, I had made it myself three years ago. But now I had a bow—a man's bow. Kanti could have my spear. Once I was beyond the view of the village, I began to jog.

"Chogan, what's the rush?" Kanti jogged along beside me. It was not as if she disliked running; I'm sure she could outrun me if our legs were equal. Kanti found a question to match every action. Jogging did seem unusual. I slowed to a walk to explain.

"I saw her again yesterday during the hunt."

"Saw who?"

"The she-wolf. We were north of Wagosh Lake. I was afraid she would be caught in our trap and killed."

"Was she?"

"No. But there was no way she could have slipped through our line. We were too close together. Someone would have seen her. I thought they would surely shoot her when she passed through the narrows between the lake and the rocky outcrop. No one there saw her—I asked."

"What do you think happened to her?" I could tell by her voice that Kanti shared my concern.

"I think she went underground. She has to have a den somewhere north of Wagosh Lake, and I plan to find it."

"How will we find the den?" Kanti had transformed the wolf project from I to we.

"I think she's hiding in an old den. Wolves sometimes use the same den for several years. A new den would have a mound of fresh sand around the hole. Someone would have noticed that. But even an old den should have a small amount of fresh sand around the edges. We just need to look harder. If we quickly check the snares, maybe we'll have time to find the den."

"Let's run," Kanti said

Kanti took off running down the trail, turning into the woods when she reached the bend in the trail. I had planned to jog between snares. Now I had to run to keep up with Kanti. As long as she was running in the right direction, I let her take the lead. She ran to the right of a large gully and then to the left around a patch of tag elders. She was quickly learning the ways of the woods.

"Kanti, slow down."

Neither of us could maintain that pace for long. Kanti slowed to a jog, but not because she was winded. We arrived at the river one hundred paces downstream from the log crossing—not bad reckoning for her second time on the trap run. She either had a natural gift for navigating the woods or was lucky.

I took the lead to ensure we avoided the dead moose. I didn't want to take any chances. The bear would stay in the area, feeding off the moose until it was gone.

We found a rabbit in the third snare. It was the second rabbit in that snare in two days. There couldn't be too many rabbits left in the area. I reset the snare anyway. By the time we reached the north side of Wagosh Lake where I had the last of the snares, we had two rabbits and a muskrat.

Running from trap to trap had saved time; the sun had not yet reached the top of the sky. I was ready to search for the wolf den, but Kanti insisted we eat. I would have been satisfied with dried beaver, but Kanti insisted on frog legs with her meal. Arguing with Kanti is like trying to convince a toad to fly. I started a fire while Kanti tried out her new spear. I found my old spindle and hearth board in the hollow log where I had left them two days earlier. I had barely nursed the fire into flames when Kanti returned with two bullfrogs on her spear tip. Only the frog's legs are worth eating, but we roasted the entire frog at the end of sticks and then broke off the legs to eat them. They were tasty, but hardly worth the effort for the amount of meat on a frog's leg. Kanti didn't care; she got to use her new spear.

"You ready to hunt wolves now?" I asked.

I stomped out the fire, hoping that might motivate her. Kanti stuffed the last of her dried beaver sticks into her mouth.

"You can leave the rabbits and muskrat here," I said. "We'll be coming back."

Kanti laid the rabbits and the muskrat on the log and then grabbed her spear.

"I'm ready," she said.

We headed east and then swung around to the north. I had hoped to approach the wolf den from downwind. I had seen the she-wolf on two different occasions. I was hoping for a third.

"The den will be dug into the side of a hill. Look for anything that looks like fresh dirt. Talk only if you have to and then whisper." Kanti nodded in agreement. She had sharp eyes, but not talking would be a challenge.

We spent most of the afternoon inspecting every hill and outcrop for signs of fresh digging, but we found nothing other than wood ticks and black flies. The wolf had to be somewhere. The sun was getting low in the western sky. Much as I hated to admit it, the wolf had eluded us.

"Kanti, it's getting late. We need to head back."

I knew Kanti was disappointed, but Mother would worry if we were not back soon. We could try again some other day. I could see the tall spruce on the north shore of Wagosh Lake in the distance and headed toward it. We still needed to pick up our rabbits and muskrat.

"Look, Chogan," Kanti whispered. She pointed to the gray figure in the distance. "She caught a muskrat." The she-wolf was running away from the lake with a muskrat in her mouth.

"More likely she stole our muskrat," I said. I held my hand in front of Kanti as a signal to stop. "Watch and see where she goes."

The wolf disappeared into a thicket on the side of a hill not far from the lake. I waited for her to emerge. She either had a den dug into the side of the hill or was hiding in the thicket waiting for us to leave.

"Come on; let's see if she has a den in there." We cautiously approached the thicket. Wolves avoid people when given a chance, but they can still be dangerous when cornered; I had no intention of cornering the wolf.

I walked around the thicket searching for places where a wolf might hide. There it was. I would never have seen the hole if it hadn't been for a patch of yellow sand around the entrance. It wasn't much. As I had expected, the den was old and weeds had grown over the old dirt.

"Kanti, there's her den. We've found it." Kanti ran over to look.

"Yuck, I wouldn't want to live in there."

"Did you notice how skinny she was?" I asked. "She had her pups."

That gave Kanti a new appreciation for the hole in the ground.

"How many pups do you think she has?"

"I don't know, maybe two or three," I replied. "We need to leave before we scare her."

As I expected, when we got back to the log by the tall spruce, the muskrat was missing. At least she had good taste. I also preferred muskrat over rabbit. Now that we knew where to look, we could see the den from the spruce tree. She must have been watching us all along.

"Chogan, why isn't she with a wolf pack?"

"I don't know. Something must have happened to the others. Normally, the pack would provide food for the mother and her pups. That's why she stole the muskrat. She was desperate. Wolves don't normally come near anything with a human scent."

"We need to feed her," Kanti said.

"I think we just did."

CHAPTER FIVE

The Mystery Cave

"There she is...over by that white pine." I pointed toward some bushes at the base of a large white pine. At the moment, there wasn't much to see, only fleeting glimpses of gray moving among the brush. That would soon change. If she wanted the rabbit, she would have to enter the open area. Then we would see her clearly.

We left a rabbit on the log where she had stolen our muskrat two days earlier. It was the least we could do, since she couldn't travel far from her den in search of food. Summer provided us with an abundance of food; we wouldn't miss the rabbit.

We didn't have long to wait. The she-wolf stopped at the edge of the clearing and lifted her nose to sniff the air. We had been in the area so many times, our smell no longer alarmed her. She cautiously looked around and then ventured into the clearing. Fortunately for us, she never looked up at the tall spruce; eagles, hawks, and other sky predators posed no threat to wolves.

The wolf walked over to the log where we left the rabbit. It was no more than twenty paces from our climbing tree. Looking down on her, we could see glossy patches of black on her gray fur. Her eyes were deep yellow with jet-black pupils, and just above the eyes—on an otherwise black muzzle—were brown eyebrows, providing an almost human-like face. That hadn't been visible from a distance. The animal was even more beautiful when seen close up.

The wolf walked around the rabbit several times sniffing the air. I'm sure our smell still made her nervous. She inspected the rabbit from every angle. First she circled the rabbit in one direction, and then she circled the rabbit in the opposite direction. Each time the circles became smaller. Periodically, she paused, looking in every direction except up. It was a difficult choice to make, but once she made the decision, her actions were swift. She grabbed our rabbit and ran toward her den, never looking back.

Kanti and I sat on our spruce branches in silence. There was nothing more we could add to what we had just seen. We both wished she would return, but now that she had our rabbit, we knew she would remain in the den with her pups. I looked up at the sun.

"Kanti," I whispered. "It's getting late. We should be heading back." Kanti voiced no reply. She only nodded. Even after giving away the rabbit, we still had an opossum and a small raccoon to show for our efforts. We had carried them into the tree so the wolf wouldn't clean us out. Mother and Grandfather would expect meat to add to our dinner, but tonight it wouldn't be rabbit.

We climbed down the tree and headed toward our village. I let Kanti take the lead. She now knew the way as well as I did. We arrived at the river crossing dead on.

"Chogan, can we check the traps again tomorrow?" she asked, finally breaking the silence. We had been thinking the same thoughts.

"Mother and Grandfather would want to know why," I said. I tried to think of a reason for returning the next day, but none came to mind. "It would be better if we kept our routine. Grandfather won't be happy if he discovers we're giving away our catch."

"Two days is a long time to wait."

"I'll be busy tomorrow, anyway," I said. "There's a cave I plan to explore. Then I want to go hunting with my bow. I've been practicing. If I'm close enough, I think I can hit a rabbit—as long as it isn't running."

"Can I come with you when you explore the cave?"

"It's better if I do that by myself; besides, I'm sure Mother will have work for you."

Kanti walked across the log bridge using the bottom of her spear as a walking stick—not that she needed to. I followed her across hanging on to some of the branches for stability.

"Look, Chogan, there's a porcupine up ahead. I'm going to spear it."

I looked in the direction Kanti was pointing. Forty paces ahead of us, a porcupine lumbered toward a large oak. Porcupines are about the dumbest creatures in the forest. They assume their quills will protect them from all dangers. But their quills offered no protection from Kanti's spear or my arrows. Porcupines provided good meat once you got past the quills, and this porcupine was bigger than the rabbit we gave to the wolf.

"Stand back; I'm going to shoot it with an arrow," I said. It would be an easy shot.

I drew an arrow from my quiver and pulled back on my bow. With the porcupine only twenty paces from us, I couldn't miss. I aimed for its belly and released my arrow. The arrow went over its head. I just needed to get the range. My second shot would be better. The porcupine, unconcerned with the near miss, continued its slow walk toward the oak tree. My second shot flew off to the left.

"Want me walk up and stick it with my spear?" Kanti asked.

"No, I'll hit it." I was confident and I still had a quiver full of arrows. Finally, my fourth arrow found its mark. Perhaps I still needed practice.

Kanti walked up to the porcupine and dispatched it with a thump on the head from her club.

"How we going to get it home?" I asked. I assumed there was no easy answer. Porcupines don't come with handles, and I had no desire to grab a handful of quills.

"You carry the raccoon and 'possum." Kanti passed the dead animals to me. "I'll carry the porcupine."

Then she stuck her spear into the porcupine and slung the spear over her shoulder. I found that a bit misleading, since I was the one who shot the porcupine. Now everyone would assume Kanti speared the porcupine, but no one noticed when we entered the village. Porcupines are not as exciting as moose or deer.

We set our catch on the ground in front of our wigwam. Despite giving away the rabbit, it was an impressive display. Mother was steaming birch bark to make it bendable. We waited while she folded the bark into a container and set it on a rock to cool. Later, she would seal any holes and cracks with spruce pitch, so we could use the containers for collecting maple sap.

"You kids did well today," Mother said after inspecting our catch. "That's more than we can eat tonight. We'll eat one of them and smoke the other two."

"I want to eat the 'possum tonight," Kanti said. Opossum was her favorite.

"But porcupine tastes better," I said. "Can't we eat the porcupine?" I assumed being the older sibling, Mother would go with my selection. "Opossum is better smoked."

"You guys decide which you want and let me know." Mother had no desire to take sides. "And make your decision soon or we won't have anything for dinner."

Kanti crossed her arms in front of her chest in her "I'm not giving in" stance. She can be stubborn, but so could I. It was my first kill with a bow and arrow. I had no intention of giving in.

"Kanti, I'll give you my spear if you'll agree to eat porcupine tonight."

Kanti's defiant posture instantly melted, and I knew I had her. She had assumed the spear was hers; although, I had never formally given it to her. She would never part with the spear.

"If you give me the spear and take me to the cave tomorrow, it's a deal."

Adding the trip to the cave was merely for saving face; but if it made Kanti happy, that was fine with me. I had considered taking her with me anyway. We would be eating porcupine, and I hadn't surrendered anything.

"Mother, we've decided on the porcupine."

Mother looked at Kanti to see if she had agreed to the porcupine. Kanti nodded. She now owned my spear, and sooner or later, we would still have to eat her 'possum.

"Can you skin the animals?" Mother asked. "I have to finish these containers, so we can collect sap tomorrow."

Kanti glared at me. "You tricked me," she whispered. "You knew we would be tapping trees tomorrow."

"Hush up. If Mother hears about the cave, she might forbid us to go."

"But you knew all along we couldn't go to the cave tomorrow."

"I knew no such thing. I found out about tapping the trees the same time you did. Maybe if we hurried, we could hang the containers and still have time to explore the cave." Kanti didn't look convinced.

Every spring we tapped maple trees to collect sap. That was the job of the older kids in the village. With all the containers left over from last year and the new containers mother was making, we would be busy most of the day—assuming we worked at a normal pace.

"We'll start early and run from tree to tree," I said. "That should give us time to explore the cave."

"You never get up early," Kanti replied.

"You can wake me when you get up." To be truthful, I didn't know when Kanti got up, but I knew it was early. She was always up when I awoke.

"Can I wake you with my new spear?"

"Only if you use the blunt end."

"I'll start with the blunt end, but if that doesn't work, I'm sure the pointed end will."

The following morning I awoke with a spear prodding my ribs. It was the blunt end, but it still felt sharp. I rolled over to continue my sleep.

"Ouch! Kanti, that's the sharp end of the spear."

"The blunt end wasn't working."

I sat up on my sleeping bench and looked at Kanti. I could barely see her in the dim light. The business end of her spear was pointing at my ribs in case I needed further encouragement.

"It's dark," I said. "It's not even morning."

"Hear those birds chirping? That makes it morning. We're going to start tapping trees early. Remember? I want to see that cave of yours."

I had to admit, I could hear robins chirping in the background. Apparently, they couldn't tell time either. I looked over at Grandfather; he was still asleep. It had to be early.

Since it was obvious Kanti wouldn't permit further sleep, I stepped outside to assess the day. A light shade of pink in the east was the only evidence of dawn. If it hadn't been in the east, I would have sworn it was a sunset.

"I've packed as much as we can carry. We'll have to make three trips." Kanti gave me six birch bark containers and picked up another six for herself. She ran her spear through the handle loops and draped the spear over her shoulder. "Ready?" she asked.

Maple trees are not abundant along the southern shore of Gitche Gumee, but I knew a stand not far from the cave. I headed in that direction. We found a large maple along the way whose leaves and limbs blocked out the sky. The tree was so large my arms would only wrap half way around the trunk. A section at the base of the tree had rotted with age forming a cavity big enough for a large coon to comfortably nap. The tree was otherwise sturdy and would produce a large amount of sap.

"I'm going to tap this one," I said.

I held a sharpened stone diagonally against the bark of the tree with my left hand and hit it with the stone hammer. It took several blows from a variety of angles before I had a diagonal grove cut down to the white sapwood. I made a similar diagonal cut in the other direction forming a white "V" in the bark. The sap immediately began seeping into the wound and drained down to the point of the "V" where it overflowed onto the bark. I wedged a small twig into the crotch of the "V," angling it slightly downward. With the twig in place, the sap now followed the twig to its tip where it dripped into Kanti's waiting birch-bark container. She placed the container on the ground and stabilized it with a couple of stones. Mother had painted a red "V" with a solid red circle at its point on each container. This sign of a flying eagle was our family mark. Using an identifying mark on our possessions prevented family feuds. Since it was a large tree, I placed a second tap on the opposite side.

"That takes care of two of our twelve containers," I said.

"Yeah, but don't forget the twenty-four containers back at the wigwam," Kanti replied. We could only carry six containers at a time. It would take two more trips to use up all the containers—and that was assuming Mother didn't make more.

"Hey, Taregan, there's the mighty bear hunter and his little baby sister."

"I see he's tapped our tree for us," Taregan replied. Taregan and Ahanu had snuck up on us while we were tapping the tree. We should have been more observant.

"It's our tree. We found it first." I wasn't looking for a fight, but I had no intention of giving them the tree after I had made the taps. Kanti pointed her spear at the two boys in a menacing fashion. Having experienced the pointed end of her spear when she awoke me, I knew she was capable of inflicting pain.

"The great bear hunter needs his little baby sister to protect him," Ahanu said. "Come on, Taregan. We'll come back tomorrow to collect our sap."

Taregan and Ahanu turned and left. Fortunately, they headed away from the stand of maples we were planning to tap. I watched them until they were out of sight. I didn't want them following us. We walked three hundred paces and then hid in some bushes as grandfather had taught me. If they were following us, we would see them shortly. Only after we were assured we weren't being followed did we continue.

"It would be faster if we split up to look for more maples," I said. "As long as you don't wander too far away," I added as an afterthought. "Mother will have my hide if you got lost in the woods." Kanti glared at me. I hadn't meant it as an insult. Two trips on my trap line, and she thought she was an expert in the woods. "Give a good holler when you find a maple."

Kanti ran off determined to be the first to find the next tree. She had to turn everything into a competition. It wasn't long before I heard Kanti yelling, "maple." Her announcement could have been heard back at the village. I just hoped Ahanu and Taregan hadn't heard her. I headed in her direction.

"This one is big enough for two taps," she said when I approached. "You place the taps, and I'll find more trees." Without waiting for an answer, Kanti ran off searching for more maples. I didn't know who left her in charge, but it was a good plan. She was yelling "maple" before I finished cutting the second tap on the tree.

By midafternoon, we ran out of sap containers. We had been running from tree to tree, and I was exhausted. Even Kanti was showing signs of fatigue, although that didn't dampen her excitement about the cave. I feared she would be disappointed. The cave was probably nothing more than a small hole in the ground. I had only seen the cave from its mouth. I had no idea how big it was.

The cave was no more than a short hike from where we stood, but I was tired. Despite Kanti's begging, I insisted on a few moments of rest. We sat on the trunk of a white pine that had been uprooted by a recent storm and chewed on our venison sticks.

"Do you think the cave could be right under us?" Kanti asked. "Is it big enough where we could get lost?"

I thought about the question before I answered. We were close to the cave, but not that close. I had only seen the opening. I had never ventured inside. For all I knew, it could be just a shallow pocket at the base of the cliff.

"Probably not," I replied. "We'll soon know." I stood up and headed toward the cave. Kanti eagerly followed after me.

It had been over a month since I found the opening to the cave, and I was no longer sure of its exact location. It was somewhere along the base of a granite ridge that ran parallel to the shore of Gitche Gumee. A narrow strip of black rock separated the ridge from the water. The cave opening was hidden in the thick brush that covered the side of the granite ridge.

"I think it's over here," I told Kanti. I climbed over some large boulders and began searching through the brush. A month ago the bushes lacked leaves, which was how I discovered the cave. Now it was one mass of green. I parted some branches, but found only a granite wall. I moved farther along the ridge to where a scraggly oak was trying to grow out of a crevasse in the rock. That looked familiar. With a little searching, I found the entrance to the cave hidden in the bushes beside the oak.

"Here it is," I said. It was nothing more than a black hole. I could see nothing inside. The leaves were blocking the light. "We need to cut away the brush."

I began hacking away at the larger bushes with my stone chisel while Kanti pulled the smaller bushes up by their roots. I was surprised at how big the cave entrance was. After the brush was cleared away, a grown man could enter standing up. The cave was still dark, but once we entered and our eyes adjusted to the light, we could see fine. I was disappointed by the small size of the cave. It came to a blunt end twenty paces from the entrance. What I had thought were openings to other chambers were nothing more than small pockets in the cave wall.

"Wow! Do you think this cave has been here forever," Kanti asked. She was still impressed despite its smallness.

I felt along the wall. Instead of being smooth and weathered like normal rock, the walls were rough and angular. "Kanti, this isn't a natural cave. Someone made it. Feel the walls." Kanti ran her hands over the wall, not sure what she was expected to find. "See how rough it is," I said. "The rock has been chipped away."

"Why would anyone want to make a cave?" Kanti asked. "That would take forever." She now had a whole new respect for the size of the cave. "What were they looking for?"

"I don't know," I said. I began searching the cave for an explanation. In the back of the cave I found a large oval rock with a groove around its center. "This must be what they used to make the cave." I held the rock up for Kanti's inspection. "See the groove around the rock. That's where they attached the handle."

"It's awful heavy," Kanti said. "I would think it would be too heavy for a club."

"You would need a heavy club to break this rock." I continued my search. "Let's see what else we can find."

I found one more hammer head, but nothing else. Rock chips covered the floor of the cave, leaving no doubt the cave was man-made. Most of the rock chips were gray and speckled, consistent with the granite that was so common in the area, but a few pieces were green. I hit one of the green pieces with the hammer head to break it in half. I wanted to see what the inside looked like, but instead of cracking like a normal rock, the hammer left a dent in the rock. And the rock's scratched surface was now red and shiny. I had never seen a rock you could dent. It was mystical.

"Kanti, maybe this is what they were looking for." I showed her the dent in the stone and the streaks of red. We began looking for other mystic stones. A thorough search of the cave revealed only three similar stones.

"Who do you think made this cave?' Kanti asked. "Grandfather has never mentioned anything about a cave."

"This cave is older than Grandfather. That oak blocking the entrance began growing before Grandfather was born."

We had spent more time in the cave than I had intended. It was getting late and the sun was sinking in the west. "We should be getting back," I said. I was walking toward the mouth of the cave when I saw it. Near the entrance, a small green stone protruded from a pile of broken stones. It was only barely visible. If it hadn't been for the green color, I would have overlooked it. I pulled it from the pile of stones to add to my collection, but it was unlike the other stones. Someone had shaped it into a perfect arrowhead. That was impossible. Arrowheads were shaped by chipping away at the stone. These mystic stones didn't chip; they only dented when struck. The stones were enchanted. And now I had an enchanted arrowhead. I showed it to Kanti, and she was as amazed as I was.

"Kanti, I think it best if we don't tell anyone about our cave. Maybe we can find more of these stones.

Old Copper Culture

Seven thousand years ago an ancient civilization discovered copper along the southern shore of Lake Superior. Some of the copper, tarnished green in color, lay loosely on the surface waiting to be gathered. The rest of the copper remained hidden from sight in superficial veins just below the earth's surface. Using nothing more than primitive stone hammers, the ancient miners excavated thousands of open pit mines, some of which were twenty feet in diameter and up to thirty feet deep, although most were much smaller. They may have heated the rock with fire and then dowsed it with water to make the rock more brittle prior to breaking the ore loose with stone hammers. The copper these mines produced was so pure, it could be hammered into useful shapes without further smelting or processing.

Other than a few discarded stone hammers and a multitude of open pit mines, the Copper Culture people left little physical evidence of their existence. This lack of evidence has led to much speculation as to who were the Old Copper Culture people. The Ojibway people who inhabited the south shore of Lake Superior at the time of the European arrival either had no knowledge of these ancient miners or were reluctant to part with the information, and there is little evidence that the Ojibway were actively mining copper during the arrival of Europeans. Some individuals have suggested the ancient miners could have been Phoenicians, Vikings, or other Old World people, but there is no evidence to support this theory. What evidence we do have suggests the ancient copper miners were the Native Americans who inhabited the area at the time.

Please see **The-gray-wolf.com/copper/**

CHAPTER SIX

A Skunk for Ahanu and Taregan

Mother was roasting the opossum when we returned from the cave. That would make Kanti happy. We ate the meat with wild rice. I was exceptionally hungry and probably ate more than my share. After dinner, I excused myself saying I wanted to practice with my bow. It was not an unusual request, since I practiced almost every evening. What I really wanted to do was make an arrow using my enchanted arrowhead.

Several of my shafts were now cured and ready for arrowheads and feathers. I selected the straightest birch shaft for my arrow. Only the best would do. I split the stems of several tail feathers I had taken from a dead eagle and then removed some of the feather from each end of the stem. It took several attempts before I had crafted three feathered vanes to my standards. I had planned to tie the vanes to the arrow using strips of deer tendon, but all my tendon strips were dry and stiff. I placed several tendons in my mouth to soak. Once the tendons were soft, I was able to tie the feathers to the shaft. The tendons would shrink and tighten as they dried.

Before I attached the arrowhead to the shaft, I removed the green surface layer by rubbing it against a piece of granite. I preferred the shining red color. While doing this, I discovered I could sharpen the sides of the arrowhead by rubbing it against the granite. When I was done, it was sharper than any knife I had ever made from bone or stone. It made the most beautiful arrow once I attached it to the shaft. I wanted to show it to the other kids, but I placed it in my quiver instead. It would be my secret—at least for now. I wouldn't even use it in practice. Someday it would bring down a large buck or perhaps even a moose.

That night I dreamed about shooting a large bull moose with my enchanted arrow. The arrow flew straight and true, piercing deep into the moose's chest. The angry moose, with hate in its eyes, charged at me, but fell dead at my feet. The arrow had hit its heart. I was enjoying the praise of the villagers when I was awakened by noise outside our wigwam. It sounded like someone or something was knocking over Mother's meat drying rack. Grandfather must have heard it at the same time.

"Bear!" he shouted in his loudest voice. Then he yelled out a war whoop. Mother soon joined in. Moments later the entire village was yelling out war whoops from the safety of their wigwams. I'm sure people clear across the bay could hear our clamor.

Everyone stayed in their wigwams. It is safer to scare away the bear with noise, and we made enough noise to scare any bear. The noise only subsided when everyone had grown hoarse. Grandfather then ventured out and returned shortly.

"It got all our meat," he said. "It is too dark to see much else."

I wondered if it was the same bear I saw by the river. Bears normally fear men, but the bear I saw was so big it didn't need to fear anything.

"We might as well go back to sleep," Grandfather said. "It won't be coming back tonight."

I awoke early the following morning—not as early as Grandfather—but early for me. The whole village was astir. I stepped outside the wigwam and looked about our village. It looked like it had been hit by a wind storm. Almost all the drying racks were overturned. Much of the meat had been eaten, and what wasn't eaten had been destroyed. Mother was salvaging what she could.

"Was it a bear?" I asked.

"No other animal can cause this much damage," Grandfather said. "Hassun and some of the young men have gone after it."

Someday I would be joining such a hunting party. Maybe my enchanted arrow would bring down a mighty bear instead of a bull moose. "Do you think they'll find the bear?" I asked.

"It's unlikely," Grandfather replied. "The ground is dry and hard. The bear will leave no tracks. It could already be a day's walk from here."

Mother got that worried look on her face. "Do you think it's safe for Chogan and Kanti to collect sap and check their trap line?" she asked. Bears scared Mother.

Grandfather thought it over for a moment; he was not one to make hasty decisions. "Perhaps it would be wise if they waited a day before checking their traps," he said. "The maple trees are closer to the village. I think it's safe for them to collect sap."

We could have the sap collected by noon if we hurried. That would provide time to practice with my bow. We used the stomach of a bull moose to collect the sap. It had stretched over time and could now hold more sap than I could carry, if we were to fill it to the top.

We stopped first at the big maple with the hollow in the base of the trunk. Both containers were empty and had black circles marking the containers. The circle lacked imagination, but I recognized the symbol for Ahanu's family—

Ahanu and Taregan had gotten there first. They had stashed our containers inside the hollow of the trunk. I retrieved our containers and threw Ahanu's containers into the trunk hollow. Tomorrow we would have to arrive before Ahanu and Taregan.

It took three trips to collect the sap. I emptied the last load into a large birch bark container next to the fire where Mother was heating stones. Once the stones were red-hot, Mother scooped them up with deer antlers and added them to the sap. The sap sizzled violently, as water turned into steam. She would be repeating this most of the day. When most of the water had evaporated, we would have the sweetest syrup. Sometimes she would let the sap totally evaporate, and we would have sugar candy. I loved her sugar candy.

The following morning I was awakened by the blunt end of Kanti's spear. I had learned it was best to get up immediately when poked with the blunt end. Not only did we have to collect sap, but we needed to check the traps. If we were to collect the sap, check the traps, and still have time to watch the wolf, we needed an early start.

I wasn't surprised to find our containers inside the hollow trunk again and Ahanu's empty containers under the taps. We still collected enough sap from the other trees to keep Mother busy. We finished the sap collection just before noon and headed out to check our traps.

The first three traps were empty. That was no surprise. They had produced many rabbits in the past, and it was probably time to find new locations. Grandfather says it's best not to over-hunt an area. The fourth trap offered a surprise. I knew what I'd caught when we were still a hundred paces away.

"Yuck, a skunk." Kanti was good at summing up the obvious.

My whip snare had caught a skunk. The noose of the snare wrapped tightly around its belly, and the skunk was not in a good mood. The animal was too heavy for the sapling to lift into the air, but it did elevate the skunks back legs off the ground. The skunk maneuvered to aim its rear at us, but we kept our distance.

"What are we going to do?" Kanti asked.

"I don't know," I replied. It takes a long time to make the cord I use for my snares, and I hated to abandon the snare; but then, I had respect for skunks. A dead elm tree lying on the ground not far from the skunk gave me an idea.

"Kanti, help me peel the bark from this elm. I need a slab of bark."

"What do you need the bark for?"

"We're going to build a snare for bigger game," I replied.

Elm bark peels easily, and it didn't take long to separate a slab large enough for our purpose.

"Now comes the hard part," I said. "Give me your spear."

"You aren't going to get my spear stinky, are you?" Kanti reluctantly handed me the spear.

"I won't get your spear stinky." I could see Kanti didn't share my optimism. I circled around to the front of the skunk. The skunk tried to turn, but I used the tip of Kanti's spear to keep its rear pointed downwind. If it had all four feet on the ground, the odds would have been in the skunk's favor, but with its hind legs swinging in the air, I was able to maneuver much faster. I grabbed the skunk just behind the head with my right hand, so it couldn't bite me. Then I grabbed the skunk's back with my other hand.

"Chogan, are you crazy!"

"Probably," I replied. I was hoping the skunk had used up its spray before we had arrived, but it had held some in reserve. The smell was nauseating. At least the skunk sprayed away from me. If any of the liquid had gotten on me, it would have taken weeks for the stink to wear off.

"Help me get the noose off the skunk. We'll need the cord." Kanti wasn't thrilled about the "we" part, but she did remove the cord. If we didn't quickly get away from where the skunk had sprayed, breakfast, lunch, and maybe yesterday's supper would be coming up.

"Grab the bark and let's get going," I said.

"Where are we going?"

"To the big maple tree." Kanti still assumed I was crazy, but did as she was told. The air was fresher once we left the area. The maple tree wasn't far away. I kept the skunk's tail pointed away from us and half walked and half ran. I knew I was pressing my luck.

"There's the tree," Kanti said. That was good. I was out of breath and beginning to doubt the wisdom of my project. I'm sure Kanti had already come to a conclusion concerning the wisdom of the project.

As I suspected, our containers had been tossed into the hollow at the base of the tree trunk and Ahanu's containers were filling up with sap.

"Can you remove our containers?"

Kanti removed the containers and I backed the skunk into the hole in the trunk. The skunk had just enough room to turn around.

"You ready with the bark?" I asked. Kanti knelt beside me, eager to pass the bark when I needed it—she shared my feelings toward Ahanu and Taregan. I would have to cover the hole before the skunk had a chance to escape or turn around. Either event would be disastrous. I let go of the skunk and grabbed the bark. I think I caught the skunk by surprise, as it just stood there looking at me. I quickly covered the opening.

"Help me tie the bark to the tree," I said. Kanti passed one end of the cord to me and then wrapped the other end around the trunk. I tied the knot low to the ground. I was hoping Ahanu and Taregan would be on their knees when they untied it.

"How do we know they'll untie it?" Kanti asked.

I took some red mud and drew a crude "flying eagle" mark on the bark. "There's no way they'll ignore this if they think we have personal items inside." We finished checking our snares and headed home. We wouldn't know if our plan worked until morning.

The following day we took our time getting ready to gather sap. We wanted to be sure Ahanu and Taregan arrived at our tree before us. When we arrived at the tree, the bark had been removed and the whole area smelled of skunk. Our containers were untouched and full of sap. They were now useless, as was the tree. It would take weeks for the smell to dissipate.

We returned to the village with our container full of sap. I poured it into Mother's large container. I felt sorry for Mother. Our work was so much easier than hers. She would be heating stones all day to make the sap boil.

"Did you have any trouble collecting the sap?" Mother asked.

"No," I said.

"You're lucky," Mother said. "I hear two boys got sprayed in the face by a skunk this morning. They smell so bad, their parents won't let them sleep inside."

"It's too bad they have to sleep outside," I said. I was hoping for a drenching downpour.

CHAPTER SEVEN

Wolf Pups

The moon had traveled a full cycle since we first discovered the she-wolf's den. Summer was upon us in earnest, and the day was hotter than I would have liked. We were both sweating as we sat on our usual branches, waiting for the she-wolf to steal our rabbit. We made plenty of noise upon our arrival to announce our presence. That was to ensure that the wolf would be hiding in her den. We didn't want her to see us when we climbed our tree. Now we sat in silence, hoping the wolf would assume we had departed. It never took long. She would appear first as splashes of gray among the green leaves in the bushes near her den. Only after she was sure we were gone would she venture into the clearing.

"I think I see her." Kanti pulled down a branch for a better view. "I thought I saw her in the bushes just to the left of her den." I looked where Kanti had indicated, but saw nothing. "Over by the birch tree," she said. I still saw nothing. Sometimes our imagination got the best of us. More than once we had been fooled by a red squirrel moving among the branches.

"Wait, now I see her." I saw a gray patch showing through an opening in the leaves. It could be nothing more than a granite boulder behind the bushes. At that distance, I couldn't be sure. I waited for it to move, but the she-wolf was a master of patience. She would sit motionless watching through an opening in the leaves until she was convinced we had left. We waited.

I stared at that patch of gray, hoping for a twitch, a jerk, or any other movement that would prove I wasn't being deceived. Finally, the gray disappeared. "It moved," I whispered. The spot, which had been gray, was now green. She was on the move. We saw more splashes of gray among the green. Finally, her head appeared, and she lifted her nose into the wind to sniff the air. She must have been satisfied, because she stepped into the clearing and trotted toward the log where we left her rabbit. As she approached the rabbit, she again paused to sniff the air, finding nothing other than our lingering scent. She circled her quarry several times. Finally, she grabbed the rabbit and jogged toward her den. We expected she would disappear into the bushes as she normally did after stealing a rabbit.

"Chogan!" Kanti didn't need to whisper anything else. Before the she-wolf could reach the shelter of the bushes, she was ambushed by three young pups. She dropped the rabbit at their feet. The wolf pups immediately grabbed the rabbit and began a tug-a-war, tearing the rabbit to shreds.

"I count three of them," Kanti said.

We watched in silence. Normally, we only saw the she-wolf for a few brief moments when she stole our rabbit. Now she was standing in the clearing below us as a proud mother while her three pups played with the remains of the rabbit. The young pups weren't much bigger than the rabbit; yet, despite their clumsiness, they tore into the rabbit as if they were seasoned big-game predators. When they tired of the rabbit and had eaten their fill, they playfully pounced on each other. They had yet to learn fear—that was their mother's responsibility.

"I like the pup with the white foot," Kanti whispered.

A gentle breeze rustling through the tree leaves made it safe for us to whisper. The she-wolf didn't seem to notice. She was now lying on the grass, unaware of the on-lookers in the tree above her.

The pup with the white foot was larger than the other two, somewhat darker in color, and much bolder. While the other two pups stayed close to mom, Whitefoot wondered about the grassy opening, eager to explore his new environment.

Near the edge of the lake, Whitefoot discovered a frog that had the misfortune of crossing the pup's path. Whitefoot viewed the encounter as quality entertainment; the frog placed the confrontation high on its list of daily annoyances. Encouraged by its new coach, the frog leaped into the tall grass, seeking refuge. Whitefoot tracked the frog's scent to its new hiding spot where a subtle nudge from Whitefoot's cold nose sent the frog jumping again. The game was more entertaining for Whitefoot than it was for the frog.

We watched the pups play for a good part of the afternoon. Then for some reason the she-wolf let out a growl that sent the pups scurrying for their den. Something must have frightened the mother wolf. It was just as well. It was late, and we needed to return to the village.

Normally, people in our village are cheerful and noisy, but when we entered the village everyone was whispering quietly to each other. The laughter and loud talking so common in the village was absent. I wondered if someone had died.

"Hey, there's Chogan the mighty bear slayer," Ahanu said. "The village is now safe."

"But he only slays bears that are as tall as two men and has claws as long as a man's fingers," Taregan replied.

Both boys laughed at what they thought was good humor. They hadn't forgotten the encounter with the skunk. Normally, I wouldn't have allowed their insults to bother me, but their persistence was wearing on my nerves. I saw what I saw. No amount of taunting from Ahanu or Taregan could change that fact. It did make me wonder if my mind had exaggerated the bear's size. No bear gets that big.

"Just ignore them, Chogan," Kanti advised. "They're jealous because they've never been invited on a hunt."

That part was true. Both of them had seen one more winter than I had, yet neither one had been on a deer hunt. If it hadn't been for Grandfather, I wouldn't have been invited either at my age.

"The mighty bear slayer needs his little sister to protect him," Ahanu said.

That was more than I could take. I was ready to take on both of them. I turned to face them, but Kanti pulled back on my shirt.

"Chogan, they aren't worth it. Grandfather won't be happy if you get into a fight."

I normally don't have a temper, but I was angry and tired of their constant harassment. I didn't care what Grandfather would say. I wanted to bloody their noses.

"Chogan, let's go." Kanti pulled harder on my shirt.

The two boys must have decided they had pushed me too far. They both laughed and turned away. Teasing me was fun, but apparently it was not worth a fight—not today. We returned to our wigwam with two rabbits and a partridge, an impressive haul considering we gave away one of the rabbits. At another time it might have drawn praise, but Mother and Grandfather had other concerns.

"I'm glad you two are back," Mother said. "I was beginning to worry."

Mother always worried too much, but tonight she was more worried than normal. Even Grandfather appeared concerned.

"What's going on?" I asked. "Why's everyone in the village so quiet? Did someone die?"

"A runner arrived from a village to the west," Grandfather said. "Their village was attacked during the night by a bear. The bear almost killed a young girl."

Bears occasionally raided meat-drying racks during the night, but they feared people. A rogue bear that attacked people was a major concern.

"Is the girl going to be okay?" I asked.

"I believe so," Grandfather replied. "We'll know more tonight. The men of the village will be gathering around the fire to hear the runner's tale. This could be the bear you saw in the spring; but I doubt it is as tall as two grown men or has claws the size of fingers."

"My bear was probably not that big," I said.

"Perhaps you would like to join us at the fire council."

Would I like to join them! Only real men were allowed to sit around the fire, not young boys aspiring to be men. This was more of an honor than the hunting trip. I wondered if Ahanu and Taregan would be invited.

"Yes, Grandfather, I would be honored to sit around the fire."

"It's best if you listened and did not speak."

"Yes, Grandfather."

With all the excitement, I could hardly eat dinner. All I could think about was sitting around the fire listening to the runner tell about the bear attack. I had no doubt people would be telling the story around campfires in the future, but I would hear it while the story was fresh. I ate enough of my dinner to satisfy Mother and then wandered about the village searching for any gossip I might find. Everyone was talking about the bear attack, although no one knew any more than I did. We would have to wait for the council fire to hear the details. Women and children weren't allowed at the council, but they would be listening in the shadows.

Several men were building the fire. They were placing logs around the fire like petals on a spring flower. As the fire burned down, they would push the logs farther into the fire to maintain the flames. From the length of the logs, it appeared they were expecting a long meeting. Sometimes such meetings extended well into the night. Everyone would be given a chance to voice his opinion and offer suggestions.

I returned to the wigwam looking for Grandfather. He had invited me to the council fire. I knew men would question my status unless I sat next to him. Grandfather was talking to the man in a neighboring wigwam. I waited beside Grandfather until he finished talking. Then he turned toward me.

"Chogan, are you ready for the fire council?" he asked.

That was a dumb question to ask a boy of twelve winters. "Yes, Grandfather," I replied.

I followed Grandfather toward the fire circle. People were already gathering around the fire. They talked quietly, reflecting the seriousness of the meeting.

"Hi, Chogan. Are you joining us?" It was Hassun.

"Yes, sir." I tried to sound as if I had managed to squeeze the meeting into my busy schedule, but Hassun just smiled. We both knew this was a great honor for me.

Grandfather sat down cross-legged in front of the fire, and I sat beside him. Hassun sat on my other side. Sandwiched between Grandfather and Hassun, no one would dare question my right to sit at the council. More people joined us, and the circle began to take shape. I didn't see anyone who looked like a visitor. Finally, one of the village elders and a young man who I assumed was the messenger joined the circle. The messenger was Hassun's age. Like Hassun, he was tall and slender and had the muscles of an athlete.

The village elder stood and introduced the visitor. The introduction was long and eloquent with many references to the friendship between our villages. I wanted to hear about the bear, not listen to long speeches. Finally, the village elder sat down. I assumed we would now hear from the visitor, but someone passed the elder a wooden box. He opened the box as if it were filled with treasure and removed an opwaagan. The bowl of the opwaagan was hand-carved pipestone, and the stem was made of ash. Eagle feathers and porcupine quills dyed in a variety of colors decorated the stem. Grandfather smoked an opwaagan, but his opwaagan was made of wood without any ornamentation.

The elder packed the bowl of the opwaagan with a mixture of tobacco leaf and shredded sumac bark, and then lighted the bowl with a burning splinter from the fire. As he sucked on the stem of the opwaagan, the tobacco glowed red, and white smoke curled upward from the bowl. The elder removed the stem from his mouth and exhaled. A perfectly round smoke ring hung momentarily in front of him before it dissipated into the air. He took another draw on the opwaagan and produced a second ring even bigger than the first. It was the neatest thing I had ever seen. Grandfather never made smoke rings. All he ever produced were clouds of white smoke that stunk up the wigwam.

The village elder made a show of passing the opwaagan to the visitor who received it with both hands. He took two puffs with great care and passed the opwaagan to his left; it was coming my way. I had never smoked an opwaagan, so I watched carefully. I didn't want to make any social blunders at my first fire council. The men held the opwaagan with both hands, as if it were fragile. Then they took two breaths before passing it on. I would do likewise. I would blow a smoke ring bigger than the village elder's. I would just have to take a deeper breath.

Grandfather took two puffs, held the smoke in his lungs for a moment, and then slowly exhaled. That also looked impressive. Perhaps I should take a deep breath, hold it for a few moments, and then blow my smoke ring. Grandfather passed the opwaagan to me, and I took it with both hands as I had seen others do. I placed the stem in my mouth and took a deep breath of smoke. At least I had assumed it would be smoke. Instead, I inhaled scorching fire that filled my lungs down to my toes. My throat felt as if a hot coal had lodged in my windpipe. Sulfurous fumes clung to my nostrils. I couldn't breathe. I coughed and smoke came out of my nose as well as my mouth. There was no fancy smoke ring, only a cloud of smoke that lingered in front of my face, waiting for me to re-inhale with my next breath. I felt like I would puke, but I was able to swallow and keep my dinner down. At least I didn't drop the opwaagan. I passed it to Hassun with one hand, the other hand still clinging to my throat. Hassun smiled, but didn't laugh. That was more than I could say for the men on the other side of the circle.

The opwaagan made its way around the circle with each man inhaling one or two puffs. No one else choked on the smoke. I was hoping my performance with the opwaagan would not get back to Ahanu and Taregan. I would never hear the last of it if it did.

Once everyone had smoked the opwaagan, the visitor stood up to address the group. He stood tall and paused until the silence was overpowering. We were all anxious to hear about the bear that almost killed the young girl.

"Honorable men of this village on the shore of Gitche Gumee," he began. "I thank you for your generous hospitality. Unfortunately, I do not come bearing good news. Two nights ago, a bear entered our village and destroyed our meat-drying racks. That is not an uncommon experience and would not be worthy of your concern, had the bear not attacked the wigwam in which I slept. It was a mighty bear that is not afraid of men. The ash poles that framed our wigwam snapped like twigs under the bear's weight, and the wigwam fell upon us like an avalanche of snow. While I was crawling out from under the collapsed wigwam, the bear attacked my sister who had been sleeping beside me. She has yet to see her eighth winter. The bear dragged her twenty paces from our wigwam. I gave out a war whoop as is our custom, and it was echoed by the people in our village. The bear released my sister, but only after severely injuring her with claws and fangs. She will live, although she will wear scars to her deathbed."

The messenger described the injuries in great detail. They were gruesome. It made me realize how fortunate I was having fish to distract that bear on the riverbank.

"This bear," the man continued, "has tasted human flesh, and it won't hesitate to taste it again."

"Did anyone see this bear?" someone asked.

"Only my sister," the man replied. "She says the bear was larger than any bear she has ever seen, and its face was as big around as the largest snapping turtle."

A vigorous discussion developed over the size of the bear and the danger it presented. Grandfather was strangely silent during the discussion. That was not like him. He had an opinion on every subject. Finally, Hassun stood to offer his assessment.

"I thank our noble friend from the village to our west for sharing his tale, and we wish his sister a speedy recovery. As for the bear, I have no doubt this is a large bear. My cousin, Chogan, has seen a similar bear, and he likewise describes it as the biggest bear he has ever seen."

I was relieved Hassun did not mention bears as tall as two men or claws as big as fingers. I was still trying to live down that description.

"Even though this is a large bear," Hassun continued, "It is only a bear. Spears and well-placed arrows will bring it down like any other bear. I agree with our guest; this bear has tasted human flesh and has no fear of people. That makes this bear dangerous. We must destroy this bear before it strikes again. I suggest we gather hunters from all the villages into a large war party to hunt this bear. We will search the woods until we find this bear, and then we will kill it. Who will stand with me?"

The visitor immediately rose to stand with Hassun. Twenty other young men stood up. I was tempted to join them but was afraid they would laugh. Even if I did, Mother would never let me go on a bear hunt.

That must have been the end of the meeting, as some of the older men began drifting away, although the younger men remained to discuss the coming hunt. This would be the greatest bear hunt ever.

Grandfather got up to leave, and I joined him. "Do you think they will kill the bear, Grandfather?" I asked. "They will have many men to search the forest."

"Never underestimate a bear, Chogan. They are smart animals. If they don't wish to be seen, they can be hard to find."

Grandfather, who had wisdom to share on every topic, said no more. Tonight he was unusually quiet. This bear scared even Grandfather, and there wasn't much that scared Grandfather.

CHAPTER EIGHT

Whitefoot

I knew something was wrong even before we reached our climbing tree. It was that faint odor of decaying flesh. It reminded me of the dead moose we had found in the spring, although this odor was not as strong.

"Kanti, do you smell that?"

Kanti closed her eyes and sniffed the air. "It's better than skunk, but not by much. Something's dead."

I was hoping the gray wolf had made a major kill. A deer would provide food for the wolf and her pups for several days. The smell became stronger as we approached the clearing where we had seen the pups play. Kanti saw the gray wolf first.

"Oh, Chogan!"

The wolf was lying on her side with her head turned up. From its awkward position, I knew she was dead. We approached in silence. Close examination left little doubt as to what had happened. The she-wolf had claw marks on her back and chest. Two of her pups lay dead at her side. They were also covered with blood.

"Bear," I said. Kanti just nodded. The bear hadn't killed the she-wolf for food; it had killed for pleasure. Other than the claw marks and a few deep bites, the bodies were unmolested.

"How did the bear kill her?" Kanti asked. "She could have outrun the bear, and there's no way a bear could sneak up on her. She was always so wary."

"She could outrun the bear," I replied, "but her pups couldn't. She stayed to fight for her pups."

I looked around for the third pup; Whitefoot was missing. The bear had killed for food after all. It preferred the pup's tender meat over that of the mother.

"We can't leave them here," I told Kanti.

"What should we do with them?" she asked.

"We can bury them in their den. We'll push them down the hole and cover the opening. I don't think the bear will dig them out."

I dragged the she-wolf toward her den by her back legs. It wasn't very elegant for such a noble animal, but I didn't want to get blood on me. Kanti carried the dead pups in her arms. She wasn't worried about blood. Tears flowed down her cheeks. I turned away, so I wouldn't embarrass her. We pushed the animals into the den and filled the opening with sand. Then we paused in front of the den for a moment of silence. Even I was teary-eyed, although if somebody had said so, I would have denied it.

The bushes concealed the den. It was no wonder we had difficulty finding it. I had passed the den many times while checking my snares without knowing it. Now, when I passed this way, I would remember the gray wolf and her pups. I would think of the den hidden in the bushes where their bodies lay. The memories would be a mixture of pleasure and sorrow. I was about to leave when I felt pain in my right foot. I looked down to discover Whitefoot viciously attacking my moccasin. He tried thrashing it about as he had the rabbit. Fortunately, his teeth couldn't puncture the moccasin, but it still hurt. I reached down and grabbed him by the skin on his neck. It took some effort, but I pried my foot free. I held the wolf pup up in the air. He gave a feeble growl and then looked at me with sheepish eyes.

"Hey, little buddy. We aren't going to hurt you. We're on your side."

"Chogan, it's Whitefoot. He must have been hiding in the bushes."

Kanti offered a strip of venison, and the wolf pup bit into it eagerly. With Whitefoot's teeth now occupied, I could safely gather him into my arms. He probably hadn't eaten in two days.

"What are we going to do with him?" Kanti asked.

"We can't take him back to the village," I said. "Grandfather wouldn't approve."

"But we can't leave him here. He'll die without someone to care for him."

Kanti was right. Without help, he would surely die. "We'll care for him," I said. "The she-wolf would have wanted us to."

Kanti gave him another piece of venison, which he grabbed as eagerly as he had the first piece. "He's hungry."

I was glad Kanti brought plenty of meat. I'd rather have him chew on venison than my fingers; my toes were still hurting. "We need a leash for him," I said. "Maybe we can use the cord from one of our snares. That snare down by the lake won't catch any more muskrats. We can use that one."

Kanti untied the cord and let the sapling spring free. We caught two muskrats with the snare, but now muskrats were avoiding it. The cord would make a sturdy leash. I tied the leash around the pup's neck and set him on the ground. I expected him to run for the bushes, but he stood there as if he didn't know what to do. We sat on the grass beside him. After a moment he walked over and pressed against my thigh. He was scared and willing to accept any friend he could get. I stroked his fur. It was silky smooth like a beaver's pelt.

"What'll we name him?" Kanti asked. "He needs a name."

"We've been calling him Whitefoot. I suppose we could stay with that."

"I like Whitefoot." Kanti reached over and scratched the wolf's head; he responded by licking her hand. Dried meat can buy a lot of friendship; he had bitten me. She gave him another stick of venison.

"You never answered my question," Kanti said. "What're we going to do with him? We can't take him back to the village."

"We can take him to the cave," I said. "No one knows about the cave. We can sneak food to him in the evening."

"What if he won't stay in the cave?" Kanti asked.

"We'll tie his leash to a heavy stone."

Twine and Rope

Chogan and Kanti made twine and rope from sinew, leather, and plant fiber. Sinew (tendon) was used most frequently for delicate work such as tying feathers to the shaft of an arrow or stitching a cut on the skin. Sinew is the white fiber that attaches muscle to bone and is often obtained from the legs of deer and other large animals. It shrinks when it is dry and stretches when it is wet, making it a poor choice for materials exposed to the weather. But wet sinew was perfect for tying feathers to the shaft of an arrow. It formed a very tight and secure binding once it dried.

When Chogan needed stronger cord, he would cut strips from hide. These leather straps were strong and could be obtained in long lengths, but they shared the same flaw as sinew. The leather straps stretched when wet, causing knots to come untied.

For weather stable cord and rope such as what he used for his snares, Chogan relied on plant fiber, the most important of which was the inner bark of the basswood tree. Basswood fiber was harvested in the spring when sap was running. The entire bark was removed from the tree and soaked in water for several days until the inner bark could be easily separated from the outer bark. The inner bark was then boiled to soften and separate the strands. Two-ply twine or rope was made by twisting two separate strands of loose fiber in a clockwise direction and then allowing the two strands to wrap around each other in a counterclockwise direction.

Women placed the two strands on their thighs approximately one inch apart and then rolled the palm of their hand forward over the strands. This twisted both strands in a clockwise direction. Then they pushed the two strands together and pull back on their palms, causing the combined strands to rotate in a counterclockwise direction. When done correctly, the two strands clung to each other and prevented unraveling.

Please see **The-gray-wolf.com/cord/**

We took the pup down to the lake for a drink of water. Then I picked him up in my arms. This time he didn't try to bite me. "We're going to take you to a huge den," I told him. I'm sure he didn't understand.

It was late and we should be heading home, but the cave was on our way. If we hurried, there should be time to drop him off at the cave and return to the village before dark. The sun was sinking in the west when we arrived at the cave, and I feared we had misjudged our time. Mother would worry, but it couldn't be helped.

I tied Whitefoot's leash to a large rock at the rear of the cave. The leash would let him peer out of the cave, but still keep him inside and out of trouble. Kanti left the remainder of the venison. "We'll be back tomorrow," I told him. "I promise." He gave us a pathetic look when he noticed we were leaving.

We returned the following evening with more dried meat and one of Mother's maple sap containers. I filled the container with water and set it down before him. He drank half of the water. The cave was not exceptionally hot, but he had gone a full day without water. We would have to ensure his water container was always full.

After he finished drinking, we took Whitefoot down to the strip of sandy beach that separated Gitche Gumee from the black-rock cliffs. Even with the brush cut away, the cave was invisible from the beach. It was just another dark shadow among many dark shadows. I untied Whitefoot's leash, allowing him to play in the sand. I could easily outrun him if he tried to escape, but he clung to us in fear that *we* would escape. He must have suspected we would leave him again when darkness came. Spending a lonely night in a cave had to be terrifying to a young animal used to having a mother by its side.

Whitefoot pranced at our feet while Kanti and I skipped stones on the lake. My stones skipped farther than Kanti's stones, but then I was older and had more experience at skipping stones. She did have several good throws that skipped four or five times.

When we tired of skipping stones, we dug holes in the sand. The holes filled with water seeping in from Gitche Gumee. Then we made elaborate structures with the wet sand we removed from the holes. Mine was a cliff similar to the black rocks looming up behind us. I cut a deep cave into the side of my cliff. Kanti build a village filled with wigwams with her wet sand. Whitefoot watched our activity with keen interest, unaware that our actions achieved no useful purpose. Finally, when he could restrain himself no longer, he trampled through Kanti's sand village like some mythical beast, destroying wigwam after wigwam with paws that were far too big for such a small wolf.

Once he was assured he had left no survivors in Kanti's village, he waddled over with equal enthusiasm to inspect my creation. He was mostly interested in the cave. He inserted his muzzle into the opening in search of unusual smells. The cave, which was already tenuous, collapsed on his inquisitive nose. Startled by this sudden insult, he stepped backward and fell into the water-filled hole. He landed on his back, and for a moment I feared for his safety, but he rolled over and sneezed the water from his nose as if he had planned the maneuver and then climbed out of the hole. I found the whole episode humorous until Whitefoot shook his fur, showering us with sand and water.

"Chogan, it's getting late."

I looked up at the sky. Kanti was right. The sun was low in the west. We would have to hurry if we were to be back in the village before dark. We were having so much fun, I had forgotten the time.

"Well, Whitefoot, I hate to tell you this, but it's time to return to your cave." I tied the leash around his neck and picked him up. He gave a pathetic whine, making me feel evil and cruel. "I'm doing this for your own good," I reminded him. I wished he could understand me. It would've made it so much easier.

I tied his leash to his rock while Kanti filled his water dish. We left enough food to last until we returned the following evening. We were doing everything we could to help him, but it was still painful leaving him in the cave. "Good bye, Whitefoot," I said.

***

Five days had passed since we found Whitefoot in the clearing—or should I say he found my moccasin. No one in the village knew we were hiding him in the cave, and that was how we preferred to keep it. I didn't know how much longer that would last. We snuck food to him in the evenings and sometimes in the afternoon if time permitted. On the days when we didn't check snares and didn't have a rabbit to offer, we brought dried meat. Mother must have thought our appetites had increased remarkably. I was hoping Grandfather would think likewise.

Our biggest fear was not Mother or Grandfather, but Ahanu and Taregan. They hadn't forgotten the skunk episode and were eager to get even. There was little harm they could inflict upon us within the village other than hurl insults, which they did with increasing frequency. I had no doubt they preferred to catch us outside the village where there were no inquisitive eyes to document their evil deeds. Although they didn't scare me, I feared what they might do if they found Whitefoot. I had seen them kill animals for the fun of it. Grandfather says we need to kill animals for food, but we should never kill for pleasure.

Hassun had given us a young doe he had shot earlier in the day, and I was cutting the meat into strips for Mother's drying rack. I left an excess of meat on the leg bone and, when no one was looking, I wrapped the bone in a woven cattail mat. Tonight Whitefoot would have a fresh bone to chew on. Mother would never know the difference. She had plenty of meat for the drying rack as well as meat to roast for the evening meal. And it turned out to be a very tasty meal. In addition to the venison, Mother had fixed boiled ground nuts, sliced puffball mushrooms fried in venison grease, and wild onions. This was washed down with a red tea she had made by boiling sumac berries in water. She sweetened the tea with some of the maple syrup we made in the spring.

"That was a good meal, Mother," I said. I rubbed my stomach to prove the point. "Do you mind if I practice with my bow?"

Mother nodded in the affirmative. Learning to shoot an arrow straight and true was a skill needed for manhood. I had no doubt she would grant me permission.

"Can I help him?" Kanti asked. Mother again nodded in the affirmative.

I grabbed my bow and quiver and, when no one was watching, the cattail mat. Shooting an arrow inside the village was dangerous; therefore, no one considered it unusual when we left the village on a trail heading east. Once we were out of sight, we left the trail and headed toward our cave. Not wanting to leave a trodden path for others to follow, we took a different route each time we went to the cave.

I checked behind us periodically to ensure we weren't being followed. At one time I thought I saw a bush move. It could have been the wind or a red squirrel, but it also could have been Ahanu and Taregan. We turned a corner and, when we were momentarily sheltered from view, I pulled Kanti into some bushes where we couldn't be seen. It was an old trick Grandfather had taught me. If we were being followed, whoever was following us would step into the open where we could see them. We waited a fair amount of time, but no one ventured forth. My imagination was playing tricks on me. Just to be on the safe side, we repeated the maneuver two more times before we arrived at the cave; I didn't trust Ahanu and Taregan.

As usual, Whitefoot was overjoyed to see us. The only light in the cave came from the opening, and it took several minutes for our eyes to adjust to the dim light, but we could feel Whitefoot jumping at our feet. His water dish had been overturned. We needed to place rocks around the bowl in the future. As I bent down to untie his leash, the cave became dark; someone was blocking the light at the mouth of the cave.

"Grandfather! What are you doing here?"

"That is the question I should be asking you," he said. "I believe you and Kanti owe your mother and me an explanation."

"How did you find us?" I asked.

"I was the one who taught you how to track and how to hide your trail. Do you think the student is now wiser than the master?"

I didn't know what to say, but he was right; we did owe him an explanation. We could no longer hide Whitefoot or our strange behavior. I would have to tell him everything and hope for the best.

"A bear killed a she-wolf and two of her pups. We found her surviving pup," I said. "We couldn't leave the pup to die, could we? It wouldn't be right." Grandfather said nothing. He just stood at the mouth of the cave, outlined by the sunlight shinning into the cave. "It was my idea," I said. "Kanti had nothing to do with it."

"I did so," Kanti replied. "It was as much my idea as it was yours."

Grandfather stepped out of the light at the mouth of the cave and walked over to the wolf pup. Whitefoot was still tied to his leash. "This is a wild animal. It is disrespectful to keep a wild animal tied to a leash." Grandfather bent down and untied Whitefoot. Whitefoot licked Grandfather's hand in appreciation. Grandfather then picked up the wolf pup and passed him to me. "Here," he said. "We need to be going."

"Where are we going," I asked. I was fearful of the answer.

"Back to the village," Grandfather said. "And bring the deer leg you have wrapped in the cattail matt."

"You mean we can keep him?" I asked.

"For now. A wolf is a wild animal. He will need to be returned to the wild. That is the way of the forest. Later—when the leaves fall and winter begins—you will have to return him to the forest. He won't be fully grown, but with luck he will find his way."

"Yes, Grandfather."

"Chogan, what you and Kanti did was a noble deed. You have made me proud."

"Yes, Grandfather."

"But I would have been even prouder, if you would have told me."

"Yes, Grandfather."

I couldn't believe my ears. Grandfather was allowing us to bring the wolf pup back to the village. Perhaps by fall, I could convince Grandfather to let us keep the wolf pup forever. I would be the envy of all the kids.

After we returned to the village, I introduced Whitefoot to Mother. She wasn't as keen on the idea of keeping a wolf in the village as Grandfather was. We settled on a compromise in which Whitefoot would remain tied up outside the wigwam at night. Mother was worried he might get into our meat drying racks unless he was tied up. It wasn't total freedom, but Whitefoot would be sleeping at night. The leash shouldn't be a bother.

We played with Whitefoot until dark, and then when it was too dark to see well, I tied Whitefoot to a sturdy stake, while Kanti filled his water bowl.

She propped stones against the bowl's edges, so he wouldn't knock it over.

"Good night, Whitefoot," I said. "The leash is only for night. We'll untie you in the morning." I patted him on the head and Kanti did likewise. He seemed to understand that we weren't leaving him. I crawled onto my sleeping bench and pulled the covers over me. I was almost asleep when I heard the howling. I tried to ignore him hoping he would soon stop, but he didn't.

"Do something about that wolf," Mother said. People in other wigwams were also beginning to express their displeasure.

I crawled off my bench and went outside to give Whitefoot a good talking-to. The howling ceased as soon as I picked him up. "You have to be quiet," I told him. He seemed to understand. I returned to bed.

"Chogan, he's howling again."

"Yes, Mother." I gave Whitefoot another lecture. Even in the dim moonlight, I could see Whitefoot had a very repentant look on his face when I picked him up. He was finally beginning to understand.

"Chogan!"

"Yes, Mother."

"Are you going to do something with that wolf?"

Mother's ears must have been better than mine. I was sleepy enough to fall asleep in spite of Whitefoot's howling. The neighbors also had good hearing; they were yelling obscenities. I picked Whitefoot up and he stopped howling. It was turning into a long night.

Since it was dark inside the wigwam, I assumed no one could see well. I stuck Whitefoot under my sleeping shirt and returned to my sleeping bench. I was right. Mother didn't even notice. I pulled Whitefoot out from under my shirt but kept him under my blanket.

"This is only for tonight," Mother said.

"Yes, Mother.

CHAPTER NINE

The Hornet's Nest

A slimy tongue raked my face, jolting me from a deep sleep; I had forgotten Whitefoot was sharing my bed. I tried ignoring him, but his tongue probed my mouth and eye sockets, making further sleep impossible. Having Whitefoot awaken me wasn't much better than Kanti's spear point. Each had its downside. I pulled Whitefoot away from my face and set him on the ground. As usual I was the last to awaken. Kanti heard me stirring and brought meat for Whitefoot. No one bothered to bring me breakfast; I had to get my own.

"Some kids are waiting outside to see Whitefoot," she said.

"How'd they know about Whitefoot?"

"I don't know," Kanti replied. "I only told a few friends."

Telling a few of Kanti's friends was like announcing Whitefoot's arrival at a village council meeting, not that I expected to keep our wolf pup secret. I picked up Whitefoot and took him outside to meet his admirers. There must have been twenty kids waiting to see him. Kanti was entertaining the visitors with a demonstration of our magical stones. We had recovered fifteen green stones in all. She banged one of the larger stones with a heavy rock to show the kids how the stones could be bent.

The kids found the trick impressive, but not as impressive as a wolf pup. They quickly deserted Kanti and gathered around Whitefoot. Most of them had never seen a wolf. I held Whitefoot out so everyone could pet him. Fortunately, Whitefoot was on his best behavior and didn't bite anyone—Kanti kept his teeth occupied with dried meat. I finally had to ask everyone to leave. I had yet to eat breakfast, and then I needed to check my snares.

The kids left reluctantly, but I assumed they would be hanging around all day in hopes of getting a glimpse of Whitefoot. They also showed a keen interest in our green stones, which worried me.

"Kanti, we need to hide our stones or someone will steal them."

Kanti picked up the magical stones and placed them into a blue basket Mother was no longer using. Mother had woven the basket out of cedar roots that were stained blue with blueberry juice. It even had a tight-fitting cover. I suggested Kanti keep the basket inside the wigwam where people would less likely find it.

Grandfather had finished breakfast and was repairing our canoe. The canoe had been leaking around the seams, making it unworthy for long trips. We would need the canoe later in the summer for the manoomin harvest. Grandfather had removed the old spruce pitch and was replacing it with fresh pitch. I hated to bother him when he was working, but I had questions I needed to ask.

"Grandfather." I waited until he looked up.

"Yes, Chogan."

"You know that cave we were in yesterday?" Grandfather nodded. "Who made it?" I asked. "Someone chipped away the walls of the cave. It had to be a lot of work cutting the cave out of solid rock."

Grandfather scrapped the last of the old pitch from the canoe with a sharp stone and then set the stone aside. "Can you pass me that fresh pitch?" he said.

I passed him the wooden bowl filled with pitch scraped from the bark of spruce trees we had scored the year before. Mother had boiled it with a bit of fat to make it more pliable and then added some charcoal for color. Grandfather began beading the seams with the pitch.

"I was about your age when I discovered the cave," he said. "I noticed the chipped walls and, like you, assumed it was man made. I talked to the keepers of the stories—even the older men. All they could tell me was that ancient people carved the cave out of the rock. There was nothing in their stories that explained who those people were, where they went, or why they cut the hole in the cliff."

"Could they have been looking for this?" I asked. I showed Grandfather one of the green stones. "If you scrape the stone, the green comes off and it looks red." Grandfather rubbed his scraping stone against the green stone and it did, indeed, turn red. "I tried to break it in half to see the inside, but when I hit it with a heavy stone, it wouldn't break. The stone bent instead." After I had pointed it out, Grandfather could see where the stone had been bent.

"I have never seen a stone that could be bent," he said. "Perhaps the ancient people were after these stones. Although, I don't know what use they would be."

I pulled the arrow with the magical arrowhead from my quiver. "I think they used the stones to make arrowheads such as this. I found this arrowhead in the cave with the other stones."

Grandfather sighted down the shaft to check for straightness. Then he inspected the feathers.

Finally, he inspected the arrowhead. "You made this?" he asked.

"Yes, Grandfather."

"You have learned well," he said. "This is a beautiful arrow. I hope you use it wisely."

Grandfather ran his thumb across the edge of the arrowhead. I knew he would find it sharper than any stone or bone. "I sharpened the arrowhead by rubbing the edges against a rock," I said. "I tried to make more, but if I can't chip the stone, how can I shape it into an arrowhead? Do you know how I can make more arrowheads out of these stones?"

"It appears the ancient ones have taken that answer to their graves." Grandfather returned to repairing the canoe. He obviously had no more to offer, and I needed to check my snares.

I returned the green stone to the blue basket and placed the basket under my sleeping bench. Then I hunted up Kanti. She was showing Whitefoot to more of her friends.

"You ready to check the snares?" I asked.

"Can we take Whitefoot with us? He wants to go too."

"If you carry him," I said. "His legs are too short to keep pace with us."

Kanti picked up Whitefoot and grabbed her spear. I assumed that meant she was ready. I started walking toward our trail. I liked having the wolf pup with us, but I was worried about how he would react when we reached the clearing beside

Wagosh Lake. It could renew unpleasant memories—I knew it would for me.

"Look, Taregan, there's the great bear hunter, slayer of mythical beasts, and his snotty-nosed sister."

Ahanu and Taregan stepped in front of us, blocking the trail. Kanti lowered her spear until it pointed at Ahanu's chest—even I knew better than to call Kanti a snotty-nosed sister while she's holding her spear. I pushed her spear aside.

"We don't want any trouble," I said. "We just want to check our snares."

"That's good, 'cause we don't want any trouble either." Taregan walked up to me until his nose was a finger's breadth from my nose. "I understand you have a gift for us."

I stood my ground, but didn't reply. I had no idea what he was talking about. Whatever it was, it was unlikely to be in my best interest. I was sure he hadn't forgotten the skunk. A bit of the odor still clung to him. He finally backed off a bit.

"We want that blue basket filled with those magic stones," he said. "And you're going to give it to us if you know what's good for you." He gave me a shove that almost knocked me over. Kanti's spear again pointed at his chest.

"I don't have it with me."

"Get it." Taregan gave me another shove. "If you don't give it to us by tomorrow, we're going to smash your face."

Taregan and Ahanu stepped back and allowed us to pass. They were unaware of the special arrow in my quiver, or they would have taken it. As far as I knew, only Kanti and Grandfather knew of the special arrow. We hurried down the trail until we were out of their sight and hearing.

"What're we going to do?" Kanti asked.

"I'm not giving them our stones."

"Right, and I'll have to live with a brother with a smashed in face. Remember, there are two of them and only one of you. Of course, if you let me, I would gladly spear one of them in the leg. That would even the odds."

"Grandfather would love that," I said sarcastically. "You know how he feels about fighting."

"So..." Kanti gave me that demanding look of hers. "What are you going to do?"

"I don't know. I'll think of something."

I wasn't optimistic about tomorrow's outcome; but for now, we had snares to check. We continued down the trail. Kanti set Whitefoot on the ground to see if he could keep up with us—he didn't even try. He would rather explore everything within reach of his nose. He sniffed here and there. If a cricket came into view, that also needed evaluation. Kanti picked him up as a lost cause, although she set him down whenever we stopped to reset one of the snares. Whitefoot took keen interest in the project, especially when there was a rabbit or partridge caught in the snare.

"I think he'll be a natural hunter when he grows up," I said. "He likes rabbits and partridges."

"Yeah, but he won't find the rabbits caught in snares when he's on his own. We'll have to teach him how to hunt."

Kanti was right. We would have to teach him to hunt before we turned him loose in the fall. I had no idea how we would do that. I was hoping that would be a natural instinct.

It was just past noon when we arrived at our last snare. It was near Wagosh Lake where we found Whitefoot. It brought back unpleasant memories. So far, Whitefoot didn't seem to care.

Some animal had tripped the snare, but evaded the noose. That wasn't unusual; animals have quick reflexes. Only one in three tripped snares produces a catch. Hopefully, the next animal wouldn't be so lucky. I bent the sapling down to reset the snare, but before I could reposition the trip stick, a hornet landed on my hair. I batted it away as best I could. That produced only temporary relief. Two hornets replaced the one I chased away. Soon there were more hornets swarming around my head than I cared to count. I grabbed Whitefoot and ran for cover. I didn't stop running until Whitefoot and I were fifty paces from the snare. I was prepared to run farther if needed, but the hornets were no longer following me. It was a wonder I hadn't been stung.

"Must be a hornet's nest over there," I said.

Kanti was consumed with laughter. You can't expect sympathy from a kid sister. I suppose my fast exit did present a comical sight. I passed Whitefoot to Kanti and slowly returned to my snare. It didn't take long to discover the source of the airborne assault. A large hornet's nest hung from a tree branch no more than five paces from my snare. It was the size of a fat muskrat and shoulder high from the ground. A swarm of hornets in combat mode still circled the nest looking for victims to punish. That created a problem. The snare was in an excellent location, but there was no way I could reset the snare with those hornets standing guard. I decided to ignore the snare.

Since we were already close to the lake, we walked down to our climbing tree to eat our lunch. Neither of us had any desire to climb the tree. The climbing tree would never be the same, now that the she-wolf was gone. We sat on our log and ate our dried meat, saving some of it for Whitefoot. Whitefoot, as always, ate the food greedily. At the rate he was growing, he wouldn't be a pup much longer. We waited while Whitefoot drank his fill from the lake, and then headed home.

Mother had a dinner of squash and venison waiting for us on our return. The venison was good, but I'm not fond of squash. I still ate enough to make Mother happy. After dinner, Kanti and I slipped out of the village to practice with my bow. Not only did I need the practice, but a confrontation with Ahanu and Taregan was less likely outside the village. I still didn't know what I would do when they approached me in the morning.

We found a secluded spot along the shore of Gitche Gumee where Whitefoot could play in the sand and I could shoot my arrows against a sand dune. My arrows were less likely to break if I missed my target and hit the sand dune—not that I often missed my target. I was getting pretty good as long as the target didn't move. I even hit my target three times in a row, and that was without using my best arrows. I seldom used my best arrows in practice for fear they might break. And I never used my special arrow. That I would reserve for bringing down a large buck or bull moose. I continued practicing until my arm grew sore and I had destroyed all my targets. The sun had already set when we headed back to the village. It was past our bedtime, and Mother would be worried.

Grandfather was sleeping on his bench when we arrived at our wigwam, but Mother was still up. As I had expected, she was not happy with us coming home after dark. She tends to worry. We listened to her stern lecture and then headed for our sleeping benches. The blue basket remained hidden under my bench where I left it. I lifted the lid to ensure the stones were still there. They appeared untouched.

I lay down on my bench, picked up Whitefoot, and pulled the cover over both of us. Mother no longer cared if Whitefoot slept inside the wigwam. The wolf pup licked my face and settled down to sleep. He found it easy to sleep, but I was still worried about Ahanu and Taregan.

I lay on my bench until I heard Mother and Grandfather breathing deeply. I assumed Kanti was also asleep—she falls asleep quickly. I reached under my bench for the blue basket and quietly dumped the stones onto the ground. I listened again; Mother and Grandfather were still breathing deeply. I picked up Whitefoot and the basket and slipped out of the wigwam. A half-moon hung high in the sky. Hopefully, that would provide sufficient light for what I had to do.

"Chogan, where are you taking my stones?" Kanti whispered. I had thought she was asleep.

"Since when did they become *your* stones?"

"Okay, where are you taking our stones?"

"I'm not taking our stones anywhere. They're still in the wigwam under my bench. See...The basket is empty." I removed the lid and turned the basket upside down to prove my point.

"Then where are you going?"

"Nature called and I had to get up and take care of it. Do you mind?"

"And you need the blue basket for that?" Kanti asked.

"Look, Kanti," I whispered. "I have something I have to do. I'll be back before Mother and Grandfather wake up."

"Take me with you."

"No!"

"I'll tell Mother."

Kanti had her arms crossed over her chest in her defiant stance. I had no doubt she would tell Mother. "Okay, but you can't tell anyone what we're doing."

"That'll be easy," she said, "since I have no idea what we're doing."

I let Kanti carry Whitefoot, and I carried the basket. I knew where we were going but wasn't sure how to get there. We entered the woods at the bend in the trail and headed toward the river. Little of the moonlight penetrated the thick forest, but we still found the river crossing. I knew if we now headed southeast we would run into Wagosh Lake; it was a good size lake.

It took us longer than I had expected, but we eventually came into a clearing on the west shore of the lake. The half-moon provided adequate light once we were no longer under the trees. We followed the shoreline to the north end of the lake.

"It should be over here," I said.

We easily found the snare. The hornets were quietly sleeping in the nest, leaving us unmolested. It wasn't why I came, but since I was there, I reset my snare.

"Okay, Kanti, I need you to hold the basket." Kanti set Whitefoot on the ground and took my basket. I removed the lid. "Now hold it under the hornet's nest and be ready to place the lid on it." I waited until Kanti was under the nest with the basket, and then I broke the nest free, letting it fall into the basket. Kanti quickly replaced the lid. That part needed no explanation. Darkness or no darkness, the hornets were mad. I could hear them buzzing inside the basket.

"Now what are we going to do?" Kanti asked. "You got your snare reset, but the basket's full of hornets. Mother will want her basket back."

"We'll hide the basket in the climbing tree," I said. "Come on, let's climb the tree."

I waited until Kanti had climbed onto the lower branches, and then I passed her the basket. I climbed to a few branches above her, and she passed the basket up to me. Switching back and forth, we managed to get the basket fully intact to the upper tree branches. I tied the basket to a fork in one of the larger branches. The hornets were still buzzing. It would be a long time before they would be happy again.

It was almost dawn when we returned to the village. Fortunately, we were able to sneak into our wigwam without waking Mother or Grandfather. I wouldn't be getting much sleep, but it was worth the effort. At least we didn't have to check our snares in the morning. Maybe Mother would let us sleep in.

***

When I awoke, the sun was shining through the hole in the top of our wigwam. Mother and Grandfather were awake, but Kanti was still sleeping—waking up before Kanti was a first for me. Perhaps Whitefoot licking my eye sockets was a factor.

I set Whitefoot on the ground and sat up on my sleeping bench. Given a choice, I would have returned to sleep, but today I would be confronting Ahanu and Taregan. I needed to be prepared. I borrowed some birch bark from Mother's scrap pile. She always had scraps of bark lying around. I spread it out on my bench and drew a map using Mother's red paint. I drew several small wigwams to represent our village and a line beside them for the Gitche Gumee shoreline. Another line, which was perpendicular to the Gitche Gumee shoreline, represented the river flowing through our village. I made the line wavy in the areas where the river had a rapids. Half way up the river, I drew a log to represent where we cross the river. Then I outlined a lake with Wagosh Lake's distinctive shape at the top of the map. Lastly, at the north end of the lake, I drew a spruce tree.

"What are you doing?" Kanti had awakened and was sitting on her bench. She stifled a yawn and then walked over to inspect my artistry.

"It's a map for Ahanu and Taregan."

I let the paint dry while I ate breakfast. The bark would absorb most of the moisture. It would dry quickly. After breakfast, I fed Whitefoot. I then gathered the stones I had dumped under my bed the night before and placed them in a new container. I knew I was stalling. I wasn't anxious to confront Ahanu and Taregan. The paint on the map was dry, and I was still finding things I needed to do.

"Want me to go with you?" Kanti asked. "I can bring my spear."

"It's better if I go alone," I replied. "You can watch Whitefoot."

I rolled up the map and placed it in my pouch. Then I hung its strap over my shoulder. The plan seemed so much more workable last night. I was beginning to wonder how I would look with my face smashed in. It wouldn't be pretty. I left the wigwam and headed across the village. I didn't have far to walk; Ahanu and Taregan were waiting for me.

"Yo, Bearslayer. Where's baby sister? You got no one to protect you now."

Ahanu stepped in front of me while Taregan worked his way toward my back. I didn't like the idea of Taregan being out of sight. I was beginning to regret Kanti wasn't there with her spear. That would have kept them both in front of me.

"Out of my way," I said.

"That is no way to talk to Ahanu. Where are your manners?" Taregan pushed me from behind, and I almost fell into Ahanu, but Ahanu grabbed my shoulders and pushed me back. At least they weren't smashing my face—yet.

"Where's the blue basket with the stones you were going to give us?" Ahanu pushed me again.

"Did you forget what we're going to do if you don't give us the stones?"

"You'll never get the stones. I hid the basket in a spruce tree where you'll never find it. Do you know how many spruce trees there are in the woods? And they all look alike. I even had to make a map, so I wouldn't forget where I hid them."

"Well, pretty boy, if you don't have the basket, I guess we will have to settle for your map. Where's the map?" Ahanu gave me a shove, and this time Taregan was the one who caught me.

"I ain't tellin'."

"That's not very smart." Ahanu said. "Let's see what's in your pouch."

Taregan grabbed me from behind in a hammerlock, while Ahanu sorted through the contents of my pouch. It didn't take him long to find the map.

"Well, well, what do we have here?" Ahanu unrolled the map and studied it for a moment. "I think we can find your spruce tree with this map you so generously made for us."

Taregan pushed me to the ground. "Chogan, you can be so stupid at times. Did you really think we wouldn't find your map? "Come on, Ahanu, let's get our stones."

Ahanu threw the empty pouch at me and left me sitting on the ground. I felt my face. My nose was in its proper place, and no blood was dripping from my chin. All in all, the discussion had gone rather well.

Kanti was waiting when I returned. She was relieved to find my face in one piece. "Did you find Ahanu and Taregan?" she asked.

"Yes, we had a charming discussion. They wanted to check out our climbing tree. I wouldn't tell them where the tree is, so they stole my map."

Kanti smiled. "Someday they'll discover it's not nice to steal."

"It did tire me out," I said. "Maybe I can squeeze in a nap."

"Don't get too comfortable," Kanti said. "Mother has work for us."

That was not what I wanted to hear. Since I didn't need to check my snares, I had been hoping for a day of rest—and that included a nap. I had been up all night collecting hornets for Ahanu and Taregan, and I was tired. But if the map Ahanu and Taregan stole led them to the climbing tree and the hornets, it would be worth it.

"What does Mother want us to do?" I asked.

"She wants us to gather cattail reeds."

"Why does she need reeds?" Woven cattail mats covered the floor of our wigwam. I didn't know why she needed more.

Kanti shrugged her shoulders. "You can ask her I suppose."

I found Mother outside scraping fat off a deer hide. The hide was almost ready to be stretched out to dry. "Kanti says you need a few cattail reeds?"

"I need more than a few reeds," Mother said. "We need to replace the mats on the wigwam. They're starting to rot."

Overlapping squares of elm bark covered the top of our wigwam, but the sides were covered with cattail matting. The bark was waterproof and protected us from rain and snow. We received a lot of both where we lived. The cattail sides weren't waterproof, but the water ran harmlessly down the sides. Unfortunately, cattail mats rotted faster than bark and had to be replaced every two or three years. If Mother wanted to replace the mats on the wigwam, she would need lots of reeds.

"How soon do you need them?" I was hoping we could gather them in a day or two after I was rested.

"You won't be checking your snares today. Today would be a good day for you and Kanti to do it."

"Yes, Mother." I couldn't tell Mother the reason for my exhaustion. She wouldn't have approved of our actions no matter what Ahanu and Taregan had done to us.

"Grandfather finished resealing the canoe. You and Kanti can take the canoe up the river to the lake. There are plenty of cattails at the lake."

At least we wouldn't have to carry the reeds back by hand. And I loved being on the water. Perhaps it wouldn't be such a bad day after all—as long as Grandfather fixed all the leaks. Gathering enough cattail reeds to cover the wigwam would take the better part of the day. Kanti packed our lunch, while I got the canoe ready.

Our canoe was four paces long and one pace wide at the middle. Some canoes were longer, but short stubby canoes were easier to maneuver on rivers and streams. I checked the birch bark seams, finding them all intact—grandfather was meticulous in his work.

"Kanti, I'll carry the canoe down to the river and then come back for the paddles."

"I'm almost done," she replied. "I'll bring the paddles."

I turned the canoe upside down and lifted it to my shoulders. I was glad the river was not far from our wigwam. It was a heavy canoe. I set it down when I reached the riverbank. The front of the canoe protruded into the current, but I held the rear of the canoe and waited for Kanti. She soon arrived with the paddles and our food pouches. She also had her spear and my bow and quiver. I hadn't though such weapons were necessary to subdue wild cattail reeds; she apparently thought otherwise. Whitefoot bounced eagerly at her feet. He was ready for any new adventure.

"We ready?" I asked.

Kanti climbed into the front of the canoe and knelt on a moose-skin pad. Whitefoot claimed a spot at the very front where he thought the view was best. I waited until Kanti was settled, and then I pushed the canoe into the current and climbed into the back. We stroked the water with our paddles, pushing the canoe upstream.

Water from a shallow lake to the south fed our river. In the spring, when the snow was melting, paddling upstream would have been impossible. Now the water was low, and we had to walk our canoe through the shallow portions of the river. Making our way upstream was hard work for Kanti and me, but not for Whitefoot. He ran from one end of the canoe to the next, stopping only occasionally to place his front paws on the edge of the gunwale for a better view. At one point his eagerness got the best of him, and he tumbled into the water. I scooped him out of the water and returned the drenched wolf to the canoe. That didn't dampen his enthusiasm, nor reduce his caution. Either he had no fear of the water or he was a slow learner.

Wigwams

Indians of the Great Lakes Region built a variety of shelters. When they needed a quick refuge, they built conical, wedge-shaped, or lean-to shelters, but for winters and extended use, they preferred the oval-shaped wigwam. The gently sloping roof of the wigwam provided greater strength, yet was sufficiently flat to allow the accumulation of insulating snow. The domed shape of the wigwam also maintained heat better than the cathedral ceilings of the conical or wedge-shaped lodges.

The Ojibway Indians inserted long saplings into the ground at two-foot intervals to form the wigwam's framework. The saplings arched over the top of the wigwam until they overlapped with matching saplings from the opposite side. They then bound the ends of the overlapping poles together using the inner bark from basswood trees or milkweed twine. After a series of parallel arches defining the shape of the wigwam was in place, they added a second set of parallel arches perpendicular to the first set. Horizontal poles strapped to the sides provided additional strength.

A patchwork of birch, ash, or elm bark covered the roof, except for a small hole in the center which was left open. This allowed smoke from a fire in the center of the wigwam to escape. Cattail mats frequently covered the sides, although the Ojibway Indians often used bark for both roof and sides. Lastly, ropes thrown over the wigwam and lashed to stakes held everything in place.

A wigwam normally housed a family unit of four to six people who slept on benches along the inside walls of the wigwam. When not used for sleeping, the benches provided sitting or table space.

Please see **The-gray-wolf.com/wigwams/**

It was still early in the morning when we reached the lake. It wasn't a large lake, but cattails covered the shoreline, and that was why we were here. There were enough cattails to repair the wigwams of several villages. I pointed the canoe to the closest patch.

"I'll steer the canoe and you can pull up the reeds."

Kanti began pulling up the cattail reeds, but they were so thick it wasn't necessary to steer the boat. I set my paddle in the boat and began pulling the reeds. Tugging on the reeds pulled the canoe closer to more reeds. With so many cattail reeds, it didn't take long to fill the canoe. We tossed the reeds into the center of the canoe, while Whitefoot dodged them the best he could. He seemed to enjoy the game.

We cleaned out that patch and moved to another. The reeds piled up in the center of the canoe, almost to overflowing. We were lucky they were light. Otherwise they would have capsized our canoe. Whitefoot climbed to the top of the pile to survey his domain, but slipped on the reeds and tumbled back down, coming to a rest at my feet. I picked him up. "Whitefoot, you're getting heavy," I told him. He had grown a lot in the two weeks we had him. He would soon be a big wolf.

"Chogan, I see a fish. I think it's a bass. Paddle the canoe to the left. I'm going to spear it."

I looked where Kanti was pointing and saw a dark object in the shallow water. It wasn't as big as the trout I speared in the spring, but it was still a large fish. I eased the boat toward the bass. When we were still five paces from the fish, it must have seen us, because it swam away from our canoe.

"You'll have to throw the spear. You'll never get close enough to stab it." I paddled after the fish until it again came into view, not that it did us much good. Each time we got within five paces of the fish, it swam away. I continued stalking the fish. As long as it stayed in shallow water, we had a chance. I tried to keep the canoe between the fish and deep water.

"There it is," Kanti said. "I see it again." Kanti threw her spear at the fish, but it didn't come close. Even if she hit the bass, at that distance the spear lacked the power to pierce its scales. We needed to get closer. I paddled the canoe over to the spear, so Kanti could retrieve it.

"I'll approach it from the east," I said. "Maybe if we have the sun at our backs, the fish won't see us." I didn't know if it would work or not. I knew I had difficulty seeing when I looked into the sun.

We found the fish and I circled around until the sun was behind us. Instead of paddling the canoe and making waves, I pushed my paddle against the lake bottom. We eased forward. The fish was stationary, partially hidden under a lily pad. I approached it slowly this time. It was a huge bass.

They weren't as tasty as trout, but they were still good when smoked.

"Wait until we get real close," I said.

Kanti raised her spear and held it motionless above the water while I maneuvered toward the fish. Approaching with the sun to our back was working. We had never gotten this close before. Kanti wasn't noted for her patience, but she held back on her spear. Whitefoot watched from his perch on top of the reed pile. When the fish was no more than an arm length from the tip of her spear, Kanti threw the spear with all her might. The water exploded, drenching us with spray.

"You got him, Kanti!"

I couldn't see the fish, but Kanti's spear was swimming toward deeper water. I paddled after it. The spear slowed and then stopped. Kanti grabbed the end of the spear and lifted the fish out of the water. It was such a large bass, I feared the spear might break. Kanti swung the fish over the canoe and dropped it on the reeds. Whitefoot immediately attacked it, but when the fish flopped around the boat, the wolf pup ran for the safety of my feet; he was obviously better at hunting rabbits.

"Chogan, I speared a fish!"

Other than frogs, Kanti had never speared anything. She had a right to be proud. Few boys her age had ever speared a fish that large—and she was a girl! Mother would be proud. Grandfather would just shake his head, but I knew he would also be proud. I placed the fish at the bottom of the boat under the reeds where the cold lake water would work its way through the birch bark to keep the fish cold.

We had filled the canoe with cattail reeds and could return to the village, but mother might find more work for us. With so little sleep, it was difficult keeping my eyes open. I paddled the canoe into a stand of cattails that would keep our canoe from drifting.

"Kanti, I'm taking a nap."

Kanti was also tired; she offered no complaints. The reeds provided a comfortable mattress. I lay down and closed my eyes. Whitefoot curled up beside my face. He hadn't slept much either.

Sleep came quickly. I dreamed I was hunting in the woods with Whitefoot, but he was now fully grown. We were tracking a bull moose with antlers so wide I would be unable to touch both tips. I searched for broken branches or disturbed twigs that would suggest a bull moose had passed this way. Whitefoot had the advantage: he could use his nose. We tracked the moose through swamps and thick forest. Finally, we found him. It was the biggest moose I had ever seen. The moose turned to face us. He had fire in his eyes and a fierce look on his wrinkled face. He lowered his antlers, preparing to charge. This was it. It was the moose or me. Whitefoot nipped at his heels to divert the moose's attention while I pulled my magic arrow from its quiver. I had to place all my faith in the magic arrow, but I knew the arrow wouldn't fail me. I pulled back on the bow string and pointed the arrow at his chest. I released my grip on the bowstring and sent the arrow flying. It flew true as I knew it would. It pierced the moose's heart and the bull moose fell at my feet.

"Chogan, wake up," Kanti whispered.

It was a wonderful dream. I had no desire to wake up and abandon such a lovely dream. When I dragged the moose into camp, I would be a hero. Grandfather would be proud of me and Whitefoot. Perhaps he would let me keep Whitefoot forever.

"Chogan, wake up."

I felt the blunt end of a spear poking at my ribs. I knew what always followed the blunt end of Kanti's spear. "What do you want?" I asked. "I was trying to sleep."

"Hush up," Kanti whispered. "You'll scare them."

There is nothing worse than going to sleep thinking you are alone and waking up having to worry about *them*. "Who's them?" I asked. The canoe was still wedged in a cattail patch, which limited our view of the lake. I couldn't see anything of concern.

Kanti carefully spread the cattail reeds. "They must have flown in while we were sleeping," she said.

I looked where Kanti was pointing. Six geese were swimming in the lake not far from our canoe.

Several of them were feeding off the bottom with only their tail feathers protruded above the surface.

"Do you think I could spear one of them?" Kanti asked.

Kanti's success with the bass must have gone to her head. There was no way we could sneak up on geese. They were twenty paces away, too far for Kanti to throw her spear. And once we left the shelter of the cattails, the geese would be airborne within seconds.

"They're too far away for a spear," I said, "but maybe I could shoot one with an arrow."

I wasn't optimistic. I had hit smaller targets at that distance in practice, although not always on the first shot. These geese would not wait for a second shot. If I were to get a clear shot, I would have to shoot over the cattails. That would mean exposing myself. This was the perfect time to use my magic arrow, but if I missed, I could lose the arrow forever. I selected a different arrow from my quiver.

"I'll have to get out of the canoe," I whispered. "It's too unsteady when I stand."

I climbed out of the canoe, and my feet sank into the mud. The water came up to my knees. I notched my arrow onto my bow string and crept toward the edge of the cattails, keeping my head low. I could see the geese through gaps in the reeds, just enough to establish their positions. I would aim at the closest goose. I crouched down and waited. As soon as I stood up, they would see me and take to the air. But they were feeding off the lake bottom. If I waited for the closest goose to flip its tail up to feed, it wouldn't see me when I stood up. I timed them. Their heads remained under water for about five of my breaths. That wouldn't give me much time. I waited.

I was beginning to think my goose had lost interest in the food on the lake bottom. Finally, its tail flipped into the air—the goose was feeding on the bottom. I began counting my breaths. I stood up on breath number one, and the geese immediately took to the air, all except the goose with its head under water. On breath two, I pulled back on the bowstring. The goose continued feeding, unaware its friends had taken to flight. On breath three, I aimed my arrow at the goose. At twenty paces, the arrow would require a slight arch in its path. I aimed just above its tail. On breath four, I momentarily held my breath as Grandfather had taught me. I released my grip on the bowstring and watched the arrow fly through the air. The goose lifted its head out of the water as I was exhaling breath number five. The goose saw me and spread its wings to fly just as the arrow plowed into its breast.

"I got him! Kanti, I shot the goose!" I couldn't remember when I was more excited. I shot the porcupine, but that was at close range, and it still took several shots. I climbed back into the canoe and grabbed my paddle. "We need to reach the goose before it gets away." I didn't need to worry;

the goose was dead when we reached it. The arrow had pierced its heart. The goose died instantly. I hauled the goose into the boat.

"That's a nice goose, Chogan. Almost as good as my bass."

Kanti was not about to let my goose diminish her accomplishment. I was proud of my goose, but I was also proud of my sister, although I would never tell her that. Not many girls her age could spear a bass. I let Kanti's bragging pass without comment.

"We need to head back." The sun had passed the midpoint in the sky. We had slept through most of the afternoon. We also got too much sun; my skin was beginning to burn. Our canoe was filled with cattail reeds, a large bass, and a plump goose. That's what I called a productive day.

"Do you think Ahanu and Taregan found the hornets?" Kanti asked.

"I don't know. I suppose we will find out when we get back."

We entered the river, leaving the lake behind us. With the current now flowing in our favor, we moved quickly downstream. It was late afternoon when we pulled our canoe up the riverbank. Mother had painted our flying eagle symbol on the canoe's bow, so everyone would know it was ours.

We left the cattail reeds in the canoe—we could get them later. The goose and bass were more important. As I expected, Mother and Grandfather were impressed with our catches, although Mother was more impressed with our sunburns.

"I should never have sent you two out on the lake on such a sunny day," she said. "Let me put some fish oil on you."

"I'm okay," I said. "Really, it doesn't hurt." Mother thought fish oil was good for any skin ailment. If she had her way, we would smell like Kanti's dead fish.

"I'm okay too," Kanti said. She shared my view on the merits of fish oil.

"I suppose it could be worse," Mother said. "Two of the village boys were climbing a tree and ran into a hornet's nest. I saw one of them. His eyes were swollen shut and his lips were so puffed up he could hardly talk. He sure looked miserable."

"That's too bad," I said. "Running from hornets must be difficult when you're up in a tree."

CHAPTER TEN

A Rabbit for Whitefoot

I could feel the blunt end of Kanti's spear probing my ribs, but I was too sleepy to care. I was having this fantastic dream about Grandfather's land without trees. I could see those magnificent purple hills he always talked about. They reached up to kiss the sky, and the tops of the hills were covered with snow, just like he said. There was no way I could abandon such a beautiful dream. I knew Kanti wouldn't use the sharp end of her spear. She might have used it on Ahanu or Taregan, but not on her brother. That was all bluff. I rolled over and returned to my dream.

"Ouch! Kanti, that hurts."

"Time to get up. Mother wants us to gather firewood."

"I'm awake," I said, although I wasn't sure. I reached down to scratch Whitefoot's head. He was now too big to sleep on the bench. He had grown during the summer and now barely fit under my sleeping bench.

"I said I was up."

Kanti hovered over me with her spear pointing at my ribs like she didn't trust me. "I want you up, up," she said. "I want you sitting up."

I sat up on my sleeping bench, and Kanti lowered her spear. Still half asleep, I propped my elbows against my knees to keep from falling over. Whitefoot took advantage of the situation by licking my eye sockets. He may be half grown, but he still enjoyed licking my eye sockets in the morning.

I grabbed a bite to eat and said good morning to Mother and Grandfather. They had already eaten breakfast. Everyone in the village had probably already eaten breakfast.

"Can you and Kanti gather some firewood for me?" Mother asked.

"Yes, Mother," I replied. "I know where there is a fallen tree with dead branches we can break loose."

"I don't need much. Just enough for cooking."

"Yes, Mother." That was good. We needed to check our snares. I finished my breakfast and looked over at Kanti who was waiting patiently.

"You about ready?" I asked, as if I had been waiting all morning for her to get ready. She just glared at me. Apparently, she didn't think the dead wood would be dangerous—she didn't have her spear.

We headed toward the trail that would take us to the fallen tree. I figured if we each gathered an armful of firewood, Mother would be happy. The tree had fallen two years ago and was quite dry. We easily broke off the branches. I gave Whitefoot a stick to carry, but he showed no interest; we were on our own. After each of us had gathered an armful of firewood, we headed toward the village. No sooner had we entered the village when I heard Ahanu call from behind us. I hated the sound of his voice.

"Look, Taregan, the great bear slayer brought us firewood. That was nice of him."

"So has his baby sister." Taregan sniffed the air. "But I think baby sister needs her diaper changed."

I was glad Kanti didn't have her spear; I hate bloodshed. I tried ignoring Ahanu and Taregan, but they stepped onto the trail, blocking our path. I found their presence intimidating, but Whitefoot didn't. He snarled at them and bared his fangs; Whitefoot could be frightening when aggravated. He had a good set of teeth and appeared ready to use them. Ahanu and Taregan backed off, allowing us to pass.

"Good wolf," Kanti said.

She patted him on the head and gave him a piece of dried meat. We always rewarded

Whitefoot with a treat whenever he growled at Ahanu and Taregan. They didn't respect us, but they sure respected Whitefoot's teeth. Whenever Whitefoot was with us, which was always, Ahanu and Taregan did nothing more than hurl insults from a distance. That I could live with.

Ahanu and Taregan were the only ones who still teased me about my big bear story. Since it hadn't raided any villages for several months, everyone else had forgotten the bear. Grandfather said the bear probably left the area.

We walked slowly past Ahanu and Taregan as if we were fearless. And we were, as long as Whitefoot kept them under his watchful eye. We stacked the firewood against the wigwam.

"Will that be enough?" I asked. Mother nodded. I grabbed my bow and quiver while Kanti got her spear. We didn't want to give Mother time to suggest other chores. We headed toward our trail.

Whitefoot was now too big to carry, but he would not have allowed it even if we could. The forest offered so much he needed to explore. He bounded down the trail, pausing now and then to sniff the trees or mark his scent. He turned into the woods at the bend in the trail and disappeared. We found him waiting for us when we reached the river crossing. While we walked across the log to avoid getting wet, Whitefoot splashed his way through the river. On the other side, he shook his fur, spraying us with water. We continued on.

Our first snare was empty. I needed to move it to a better location, but I could do that on a different day. We headed toward the next snare. That one was on a productive beaver run, and I was hoping for a fat beaver.

"Look, Chogan, a rabbit."

Kanti had been poking at brush piles with her spear and flushed a snowshoe hare. The rabbit tore out in front of us, and Whitefoot took off in pursuit. We knew he would never catch the rabbit, but it was good exercise, so we didn't discourage him. There was always a chance I could shoot the rabbit. I shot a rabbit once before. Whitefoot had chased it through the woods until the rabbit was exhausted. When the rabbit sat down not far from me to rest, I hit it with an arrow. I was hoping to repeat my feat with this rabbit.

"He's turning to the right," I said. When chased, rabbits run in circles, preferring to stay in areas in which they are familiar. If we knew where the circle would take the rabbit, we could run ahead and ambush the rabbit when it stopped to rest.

Kanti and I turned to our right and headed toward a small hill. The rabbit was zigzagging, trying its best to shake Whitefoot. So far, the rabbit was having no success. Whitefoot stayed on the rabbit's tail, although he wasn't getting any closer. The rabbit continued turning toward the right and disappeared behind the hill. We waited on the other side of the hill where the rabbit would soon appear. We hide behind trees and waited. We waited, but nothing happened. Neither Whitefoot nor the rabbit emerged from behind the hill.

"The rabbit must have found a hole," I said. But if it had, why hadn't Whitefoot returned? We left our hiding spots to check on Whitefoot. I feared he might have gotten hurt. Kanti ran on ahead.

"Chogan, Chogan! Whitefoot caught the rabbit!"

I turned the corner of the hill and saw what Kanti had seen. Whitefoot was lying in a small clearing chewing on the remains of the rabbit. He had chased many rabbits, but had never caught one. I didn't think he could run fast enough. Apparently, he could.

"Grandfather is going to be impressed when he hears what Whitefoot did," Kanti said.

I was sure Grandfather would be impressed, and that scared me. "I think it's best if we didn't tell Grandfather," I said.

"Why not?" Kanti asked.

"If he thinks Whitefoot can survive on his own, we'll have to give him up. Grandfather will make us do that soon enough. Let's not rush it."

We sat and watched Whitefoot eat his rabbit. It should have been a joyful occasion. It would have been nice if we could have told everybody, but we couldn't. Whitefoot was growing up, and there was nothing we could do to stop it. We couldn't forbid him from hunting rabbits. He needed to learn those skills to survive. If Mother and Grandfather should ask why Whitefoot wasn't hungry today, we would tell them Whitefoot ate one of the rabbits we caught. We wouldn't have to tell them the *we* included Whitefoot.

We flushed two more rabbits, but Whitefoot was unable to catch either one of them. Our snares produced two partridges and a raccoon. That would provide meat for several meals. We weren't heading home empty handed.

CHAPTER ELEVEN

A Turkey for Mother

"Kanti, have you seen Whitefoot?"

"I haven't seen him since early this morning." Kanti was poking holes in a piece of leather with a sliver of bone. Her feet were getting too big for her moccasins, and Mother was teaching her how to make a new pair.

"He's gone again," I said.

That was no longer unusual. Whitefoot loved the woods. Grandfather had been right; Whitefoot was a wild animal and would never be happy unless he were free to roam the forest. I now knew we would soon have to part. We had helped him when he couldn't help himself. But he was no longer helpless. He frequently disappeared during the day only to return with a rabbit in his mouth. I had no doubt Grandfather had seen him with a rabbit.

I picked up my bow and quiver. It was a good time to squeeze in some practice. I had nothing better to do. Everyone else was busy. Mother and Kanti were making moccasins, and Grandfather was in a deep discussion with Hassun about the deer hunt scheduled for the following day. I was expected to participate, but had no input in the planning. A lot was riding on tomorrow's hunt. Summer was over and the leaves would soon be changing color. We needed all the venison we could get to survive the winter. They finished their conversation, and Hassun looked over at me.

"Hey, Chogan. I understand my cousin is good with a bow."

"I'm improving," I said.

"Your grandfather tells me you shot a goose and a rabbit."

"I was lucky." I didn't want to overstate my skills. I had learned from the bear episode that exaggerations can come back to haunt you.

"There's one way to find out," Hassun said. "I know where there's a flock of turkeys. If you want, we could hunt them this afternoon. If you can hit a goose, you should be able to hit a turkey."

Hunting turkeys with Hassun was the ultimate honor. When it came to hunting, Hassun was the best. I looked over at Mother who had been listening to our conversation.

"Can I go, Mother?"

She smiled and nodded her head. Her son was growing up, and I could tell she was proud. I hoped I wouldn't embarrass the family. Hunting turkeys was difficult. I would never be as good as Hassun.

"I'll need some time to get ready," Hassun said. "I'll be back in a little bit."

I didn't know what was required to hunt turkeys. I was ready to go now. I checked my arrows to make sure the feathers weren't ruffled. I added some dried meat to my pouch. Yep, I was ready.

"Kanti, can you keep an eye out for Whitefoot? If he comes back, make sure he doesn't follow us. He'll scare the turkeys."

Kanti nodded. She had just finished one of the moccasins and was trying it on for size. It seemed to fit well. Not bad for her first moccasin. The deer skin was a little stiff, but the leather would loosen up after she had worn it a while.

Hassun returned with a basket of green leaves and grass. I was dying to ask its purpose, but that would only flaunt my ignorance. I was already feeling insecure. I didn't want to make a fool of myself by asking dumb questions. Hassun placed the leaves on a flat rock and began beating them with a stone. I failed to see how that would help us shoot turkeys. Curiosity was getting the best of me.

"Hassun, what's the purpose of the leaves?"

"They'll make you look like a tree." Hassun took some of the crushed leaves and smeared them across my forehead. He then smeared my cheeks. "Smear it on your arms."

I took some of the crushed grass and rubbed them against my skin; the skin turned green. Kanti painted the areas on my face Hassun had missed. I was already feeling like a tree. Hassun gave me a large deer skin. The hair had been removed, and the skin was filled with small holes.

"What's this for?" I asked.

"When we get closer to the turkeys, we'll stick ferns into the holes. Then when we drape the skins over our backs, we'll be one with the forest." Hassun threw his deer skin over his shoulders and showed me how it tied around the neck. This hunting trip would be far different than herding deer into a kill zone.

Everyone looked up when Hassun and I walked through the village with our green faces and arms. I felt like one of the men. We left the village on the south trail and walked past the bend in the trail where I normally headed east to check my snares. When we reached the stump of a large birch tree, Hassun left the trail and headed west. I followed quietly by his side.

We walked a good part of the afternoon. I was beginning to wonder when we would start our hunt. I had yet to see any turkeys. Eventually, we came to a small stream. Beyond was an open meadow with tall grass. Several burned tree trunks protruded above the grass. I assumed lightning had burned off the forest, and grass had taken over.

Tall oak trees surrounded the meadow. I knew turkeys liked acorns. Perhaps this was the spot. Hassun raised his hand to signal me to stop.

"The turkeys will be feeding in the meadow," he whispered. I couldn't see any turkeys, but I didn't say anything. I just nodded as if I were in total agreement.

"How close can we get to the turkeys?" I wasn't accurate at long distances.

"Getting close is the tricky part," he said. "Turkeys are smart. That's why we need the face paint and the deer skin."

Hassun began pulling up ferns and inserting their stems into the holes on the deer skin. I did likewise. Hassun draped the skin over his back and secured in place with a strap tied around his neck. Some of the ferns extended up around his head. With his green face, he looked like any of the bushes mixed in with the grass. I was hoping my ferns were equally impressive.

"We must walk crouched down with our heads low," Hassun said. "We want the turkeys to see nothing but the ferns on our backs. Only when we get close do we stand up to shoot."

I nodded. I wasn't sure I understood all that he said, but I would watch him closely. Hassun crouched low, at almost a crawl, and slowly entered the meadow. I did the same, ten paces to his right. The tall grass came up to our hips. If I hadn't known it was Hassun, I would have sworn he was a bush. He moved so slowly, the ferns on his back appeared to be waving solely by the wind. I had always known Hassun was a great hunter, but I had never fully appreciated his skill until now. I could learn a lot from him.

We had gone a hundred paces when Hassun raised his hand for me to stop. I went down on my hands and knees to expose only the ferns on my back. I had an arrow notched on my bowstring, but I had yet to see a turkey. I looked over at Hassun for further directions. He cupped his hands to his mouth and produced a sound that was every bit of a turkey gobble. I had to look twice to be sure it not a real turkey. I would have to have him teach me how to make turkey gobbles. He repeated his turkey calls a few more times and then pointed off to our left. I looked in the direction he was pointing. From my crouched position, all I could see was the head of a turkey protruding above the tall grass. The turkey was coming towards us. Hassun continued his turkey calls.

When the turkey was no more than fifteen paces from us, Hassun notched his arrow and drew it back. I did likewise. He nodded at me and stood up. I also stood up and aimed my arrow at the turkey. As I released my arrow, the turkey began running. My arrow flew straight but hit the ground two paces behind the turkey. I didn't feel bad; no one could hit a turkey on the run. That was impossible. Hassun released his arrow soon after mine, and the turkey rolled over in the grass, flapping its wings.

"You got him," I said. Hassun had done the impossible. We ran over to the turkey. It was a large tom turkey with lots of meat on its bones. Hassun's arrow had hit the turkey square in the breast. It had to be a lucky shot. The turkey was dead before we reached it. Hassun picked the turkey up by the legs.

"The next one will be yours," Hassun whispered.

The arrow offers the advantage of silence. Hopefully, we hadn't spooked the rest of the flock. Hassun had a beautiful turkey. I now wanted one so badly. We crept further into the field, almost on a crawl. Every now and then, Hassun would pause to make his gobble sound. We were half way across the meadow when I saw the red head of a tom turkey heading in our direction. I slowly raised my hand to point out the turkey. Hassun nodded. He had also seen the turkey. We remained crouched in our places, while Hassun called in the turkey with his bird call. This turkey was more wary than the last. It zigzagged, frequently pausing to listen to Hassun's bird call. We waited patiently. Eventually, the turkey came within range. I knew I could hit the turkey if it would only hold still. I drew back my bowstring. This arrow would find its mark. Hassun rose to his feet, and I did likewise. The turkey began to run. I turned loose my arrow, but it again hit the ground two paces behind the turkey. Hassun's arrow struck the bird just as it was about to take to the air. That had to be more than luck.

"You can have this one," Hassun said. He passed the turkey to me. It was a nice turkey and would provide considerable meat for the table, but it would taste better if I had shot it.

"Can we try for one more?" I asked.

"One more and then we must head back. We don't want to take too many from the same flock."

The outcome of the third turkey was no different than the first two. My arrow landed two paces behind the running turkey, and Hassun's arrow easily found its mark. I wanted to try again, but Hassun was right. It was getting late. It would be dinner time when we arrived back at the village. We picked up the three turkeys and headed home.

Even though I hadn't shot any turkeys, I was filled with pride when we entered the village with our faces painted green and tom turkeys slung over our shoulders. I thanked Hassun for the hunt and headed toward our wigwam. Mother was fixing dinner when I arrived, and Grandfather was smoking his pipe. They both looked up when they saw me with the turkey draped over my shoulder. I dropped the turkey beside our fire bowl.

"We got three turkeys," I said. Mother walked over to inspect the turkey. Turkey was a rarity in our diet and a welcome change from venison and rabbit.

"I have dinner planned," Mother said. "We'll roast the turkey tomorrow." Because of its size,

Mother would need to roast the turkey over hickory coals most of the afternoon.

"Grandfather, may I ask you a question?"

"What is your question, Chogan?"

"Hassun shot three turkeys. My arrows all missed. How is it possible to hit a target that won't hold still?"

Grandfather sucked on his pipe and then slowly exhaled. "Hassun is good with the bow. I have known only one man who was better. That was your father. Chogan, I have seen you practice with the bow. You have the potential to be every bit as good with the bow as Hassun. Perhaps even better than your father. But you must continue to practice."

"Grandfather, I can hit a turkey if it holds still, but when my arrow arrives, the turkey is no longer there."

"After dinner we will see if you can learn to hit a moving target." Grandfather leaned back and took another puff on his pipe. I assumed the discussion was over. I used the remaining time before dinner to wash the green stain from my face and skin. It didn't come off easily, but I got most of it off.

Mother had prepared an excellent dinner; still I found eating difficult. All I could think about was learning how to shot running turkeys. I was in a hurry, but there was no rushing Grandfather. He took his time eating dinner. Grandfather finally pushed the food away. I placed the strap of my quiver over my neck and grabbed my bow. I didn't say anything. I was hoping the bow and quiver by themselves would nudge Grandfather into action.

"Chogan, you have the patience of a jaybird."

"Yes, Grandfather."

Grandfather grabbed a long piece of rope and an old woven basket Mother had discarded. "Did you want to come along?" he asked Kanti. He didn't need to ask her twice. She grabbed her spear in case one of the moving targets needed spearing.

Grandfather took us down to the beach, not far from where I normally practiced. After a brief search, he settled on a scraggly jack pine that was doing its best to grow in the sandy soil. A small sand dune provided a backdrop to catch our arrows.

"Throw the rope over that branch." Grandfather pointed to a low overhanging branch. I did as I was told and Grandfather tied the basket to the rope. He partially filled it with sand to give it weight. Then we stepped back twenty paces. "See if you can hit that," he said.

I notched an arrow and pulled back on the bowstring. I released the arrow and it slammed into the basket. I was expecting a compliment from Grandfather, but he said nothing.

"Kanti, give the basket a push." Kanti did as Grandfather directed, and the basket swung from side to side. "Give it another push," Grandfather said. Kanti pushed the basket again, and it swung even faster. "Now shoot the basket."

There was no way I could hit the basket. If I did, it would be pure luck. I notched another arrow and sent it toward the basket. It missed the basket and plowed into the sand dune, as I knew it would.

"There's no way to hit the basket when it's swinging that fast," I said.

"Give me the bow and an arrow," Grandfather said.

I gave him the bow and an arrow. He notched the arrow and slowly pulled back on the bowstring. The bow looked so natural in his hands. He took a deep breath and closed his eyes for a moment. Then he opened his eyes and peered down the shaft of the arrow. He turned the arrow loose, and it hit the basket squarely. "Give me another arrow," he said. I gave him another arrow and that too hit the basket. "Another arrow." I gave him a third arrow. It quickly joined the first two arrows in the basket. I didn't think even Hassun could have hit the moving basket three out of three times.

"Can you teach me how to do that, Grandfather?"

"It will take lots of practice, Chogan. Even with practice, some people never master the technique. You must have the gift. Hassun has that gift, as did your father."

Grandfather didn't need to mention that he also possessed the gift. I feared I might be lacking in that endowment. I had yet to display any natural talent for hitting moving objects.

"What must I do to hit a moving target?" I asked.

"Take the bow and notch your arrow." I did as he said. "Now close your eyes and pull back on the bowstring, but don't release it." I pulled back on the bowstring. I didn't see how closing my eyes would help, although it couldn't make it any worse. "Now imagine your arrow leaving the bow. Watch it as it flies through the air. Picture it as it hits the target. Remember how long it took for the arrow to reach the target. You may open your eyes."

I opened my eyes. The basket was still swinging, but had slowed considerably. Kanti gave it a push to make it swing faster. I didn't need that kind of help.

"Your problem," Grandfather said, "is that you are shooting at the target." But that is what I want to hit, I wanted to say. "Watch the motion of the target. You now know how long it will take the arrow to arrive at the target, but where will the target be at the end of that time? Don't aim at the target; aim at where the target will be when the arrow arrives."

I shot at where I thought the target would be, but missed the target.

"Try it again," Grandfather said. "It'll take practice."

I fired another arrow and again missed. I didn't have the gift. I was wasting my time. I notched a third arrow just to humor Grandfather. I let the arrow fly and, to my surprise, it hit the basket. Grandfather just smiled.

"Chogan, the rest is practice. If you practice, you could be better than Hassun, perhaps even better than your father."

CHAPTER TWELVE

A Great Journey

I was having this beautiful dream. Ahanu and Taregan were stuck in quicksand, and I was the only one who could save them. I had a long pole that could easily reach them, if I so desired. It was a difficult decision. I assumed I would eventually have to rescue them, but I was in no hurry. I liked the sound of their pathetic pleas for mercy. They were apologizing for all their evil deeds past and present. Whitefoot was sitting beside me. He was also enjoying Ahanu and Taregan's misfortune.

"We promise to be nice to you," Ahanu said. The quicksand was creeping up to his chest, and his eyes were filled with fear. He held out his arms, begging me to extend the pole.

"We'll even be nice to your baby sister...I mean Kanti," Taregan added. It was tempting to let them both go and be rid of them, but Grandfather would not approve.

Much as I hated to do it, I held out the pole. Whitefoot growled. "We have to help them," I said. Whitefoot was not satisfied with my explanation and continued with his deep-throated growl. Then I realized it was not a dream. Whitefoot was standing by my sleeping bench, staring at the wigwam door. He growled again. I heard a crashing sound. It had to be Mother's drying rack falling to the ground. Grandfather heard the noise at the same time I did.

"BEAR!" he yelled.

Mother awoke and began shouting. Soon every wigwam was producing noise. It was enough to scare any sensible bear. Whitefoot growled again. Then he pushed against the entry flap and charged out the door.

"Whitefoot, get back in here!" Whitefoot had become quite independent over the past several months. He now did as he pleased, and returning to the safety of the wigwam did not please him. I heard a deep roar that shook the foundation of our wigwam. It was the same growl I had heard from the bear by the river. I was scared, but even more scared for Whitefoot. A bear that size could kill him. I grabbed my bow and quiver and headed for the door, but Grandfather pulled me back.

"There is nothing you can do to help Whitefoot," he said. "He's on his own."

At least Whitefoot was still alive. I could hear him snarling at the bear. His snarls and growls were not as deep as the bear's. I didn't know how long Whitefoot would last. A bear is so much bigger than a wolf—and Whitefoot wasn't fully grown. The snarls, growls, and grunts from both bear and wolf continued for what seemed like forever. Then there was silence. I felt like the pit of my stomach was twisting into knots. All I could visualize was the body of the she-wolf covered with blood and deep gouges. But this time it wouldn't be the she-wolf; it would be her son. I wanted to run to him.

Then I heard a deep howl. Not a howl of pain, but a long, powerful howl that said to the world, "I am wolf, king of the forest." Grandfather finally let me go. I ran outside expecting to find a seriously injured wolf. Instead, Whitefoot was crouching by the fire pit ready to take on all comers. The fur was standing up on his neck, and he was staring at the woods as if he were daring the bear to return. I combed my fingers through his fur, checking for blood. To my relief, I found none.

People began flowing out of their wigwams to inspect the damage. The bear had knocked over Mother's drying rack as I had thought, but she said she could save most of the meat. No one else reported any damage. Whitefoot had chased away the bear before it had caused much trouble.

"Grandfather, how can a small wolf chase away a bear? The bear is so much bigger."

Grandfather inspected Whitefoot until he was satisfied the wolf was injury free. It was obvious Whitefoot had earned Grandfather's respect. Only then did Grandfather respond to my question.

"Chogan, you are becoming a good hunter. You have shot a goose and a rabbit. Someday you will shoot moose and deer. But what do you do when attacked by a hornet? You run for cover even though you are bigger than the hornet. Not even Hassun can shoot an arrow into a foe as fast and agile as a hornet. The bear may have been bigger than Whitefoot, but Whitefoot is faster. He can run with the wind and nip at the bear's back feet. Whitefoot was like the hornet. The bear decided it was best to run from Whitefoot, just like you would run from the hornet."

A faint hint of dawn was visible in the east. Morning wasn't far off. It had been a long time since I had seen a sunrise. Like everyone else, I was now wide awake. I had no interest in returning to sleep. With all the excitement, I don't think I could have slept even if I tried. This would be one of the few times I would eat breakfast with the family.

Mother prepared a breakfast of wild rice laced with venison warmed over the remaining coals of yesterday's fire. It was a good breakfast, but then wild rice is one of my favorites. Grandfather was unusually quiet. I could tell he was deep in thought. Kanti naturally filled any slack in the conversation. That girl could talk non-stop. I gave Whitefoot some of my venison. Mother didn't seem to mind. I think she felt Whitefoot had earned it.

The sun was now up, although still casting long shadows. I was not usually up this early. It would make for a long day, and I was wondering how best to spend it. I had checked my snares the previous day and wouldn't need to re-check them until tomorrow.

"Chogan?"

"Yes, Grandfather?"

"Remember that talk we had in the cave last spring?"

"Yes, Grandfather."

"I told you we would eventually have to return the wolf pup to the forest."

"Yes, Grandfather." I knew where the conversation was going. Grandfather was right, but it still did not make me happy.

"Whitefoot has shown he can defend himself against the biggest predators in the woods. He can also feed himself. I have seen him many times with rabbits. It is time Whitefoot returns to the forest."

"But you said we could keep him until the fall."

"The leaves will be changing their colors any day now. We no longer have food to feed a wolf. He eats as much as Kanti. We must save our meat, so we can survive the winter. And Whitefoot needs to learn how to survive on his own before winter sets in."

"Yes, Grandfather." What Grandfather said made sense. Winter can be difficult—even for wolves. Whitefoot would need the extra time to sharpen his survival skills.

"Grandfather," I said. "Whitefoot is free to return to the forest now. He often does, but he returns. How do we force him to stay in the woods?"

"Chogan, when you and Kanti rescued the wolf pup, you performed a noble deed. You made your mother and me proud. It was the beginning of a great journey, but your journey is not over. Now you must take Whitefoot far away. Somewhere where he can't find his way back. Then you must release him to the wild."

"How far must I take him, Grandfather?"

"Take him east along the shore of Gitche Gumee. Go as far as you can paddle in one day. You can travel far in a canoe. Then sleep on the beach. The following morning you will return without Whitefoot."

I didn't like the idea of abandoning Whitefoot on a strange beach far from home, but I had never traveled a full day by canoe. That would be an exciting adventure. I always wanted to travel. Someday I would travel west for several moons to Grandfather's land with no trees. I wanted to see those purple hills that reached up to kiss the sky.

"I'm not sure this is a good idea," Mother said. "We have a dangerous bear roaming the woods. Chogan could get hurt, even killed."

"If we see the bear, I'll stick him with my spear," Kanti said.

"You have only seen ten winters," Mother said. "You are definitely not going."

"But I'm almost eleven winters old, and I can spear a bass," Kanti protested. "We'll be safer if there are two of us. And two people can paddle a canoe much faster. We'll be home in no time." Kanti looked at Grandfather, hoping for support.

"Kanti speaks with wisdom," Grandfather said. "There is strength in numbers. It is I who should go with Chogan, but I must meet with the elders to discuss what to do about this bear. The welfare of our village must come first. As for the bear, I have no fear for Chogan and Kanti's safety. The bear cannot reach a canoe gliding across the water, and when they camp for the night, they will have Whitefoot to protect them."

Kanti smiled. With Grandfather on her side Mother would eventually give in. Mother did not look happy, but she said no more.

"When would we leave?" I asked.

"The day is yet young," Grandfather said. "You could leave now and be back by tomorrow evening."

"What about Chogan's snares?" It was Mother's final protest. "Who will check his snares?"

"Chogan checked them yesterday. They'll keep for two more days."

"I'll gather some food. Chogan, you pack moose skins in case the night is cold." Kanti ran off to organize our meals for the trip. I didn't mind her coming along. But why did she always have to be in charge?

Other than food and the moose skins, we had little to pack. I wrapped my spindle and hearth board in oiled leather to keep them dry. I couldn't always count on the proper materials to start a fire being available. We would need a fire for cooking and for warmth if the night were cold. If we were lucky, I might find small game to roast.

Even with our limited supplies, it took two trips to load the canoe. Whitefoot watched with interest. Fortunately, he liked canoe rides. We didn't need him taking off on one of his hunting trips. Mother was less excited than the rest of us. She would worry until we returned the following evening.

Word that we were returning Whitefoot to the wild spread quickly through the village, and a large crowd of village children—as well as many adults—gathered to see us off. Chasing away the bear had elevated Whitefoot to stardom, and many people were hoping we would change our mind. No one felt the pain more than I, but Grandfather was right. We had to return Whitefoot to the wild where he belonged.

"Gitche Gumee can be dangerous during a storm," Grandfather said. "If the waves get high, head for shore."

"Yes, Grandfather."

Kanti and I climbed into the canoe, and Grandfather pushed us into the river. We knelt on the moose-skin blankets. It would have been a long trip without padding under our knees. I dipped my paddle into the water and guided the canoe toward the river mouth where the water emptied into Gitche Gumee. I had been on Gitche Gumee many times, but never far from the river mouth. They say the lake goes on forever, and I was eager to see where our canoe would take us. There was a big world out there just waiting for us to explore.

CHAPTER THIRTEEN

Farewell to Whitefoot

We had paddled most of the morning and were now in uncharted territory. I didn't see anything that looked familiar. Whitefoot was restless and turning circles in the center of the canoe. He needed shore time to stretch his legs. My knees were also getting stiff. A short break on the beach would do us all good. We had passed several sandy beaches, but now black rocks covered the shoreline. They were large and powerful and fought back against the waves that splashed against them. Some of the big rocks were below the water. Those were the ones that made me nervous.

"Kanti, watch for submerged rocks. They'll rip a hole in the canoe."

"Why don't we go farther from shore," Kanti said. "With the sun in my eyes, I can't see anything until we're on top of it."

I dragged my paddle on the left side, and the canoe turned toward deeper water. The water was calm, but I didn't know how long that would last. Dark clouds were brewing in the west. I didn't want to venture too far from shore in case a storm should hit, although the shore offered no refuge at the moment. Waves splashed against the boulders along the shore. There was nowhere we could approach with a canoe. The last sandy beach was far behind us.

I pulled harder on my strokes to increase our speed. We needed a sandy beach. A tailwind pushed us forward. That was to our advantage, although it also increased the size of the waves. The canoe pitched forward into one of the larger waves. The bow of the canoe easily parted the wave, but cold spray splashed into Kanti's face. Even Whitefoot appeared concerned.

"Kanti, we need to pull into shore before the storm hits."

"There's no place to beach the canoe, Chogan. All I see are rocks."

That was the same conclusion I had come to. I paddled even faster. There had to be a reasonable landing site somewhere ahead of us. I could hear thunder behind me, and gusts of wind were now lifting water from the tops of the waves and spraying us in the face. The storm was getting closer.

"Kanti, we need to get off the lake, even if it's not the best beach."

"Chogan, there's a gravel beach between those two large rocks. Maybe we can pull in there."

I looked were Kanti was pointing. The boulders partially sheltered the beach from the waves. But before we could reach the sheltered area, we had to cross the surf where the breaking waves could easily capsize our canoe. There were no other alternatives. I dragged my paddle in the water and guided the canoe toward the beach.

"Watch for rocks," I said.

Kanti stopped paddling and leaned over the bow of the canoe. "Looking good so far," she said. She held her paddle in front of her in case she needed to push off from a nasty rock. I put more effort behind my paddle to speed us through the surf. I was thinking we would make it when a wave broke behind me. It lifted the rear of the canoe and then sent us sideways toward the gravel beach at a faster speed than I desired.

"ROCK!" Kanti shouted. She pushed at the submerged boulder with her paddle, but there was little she could do. The canoe plowed into the rock, throwing us into the water. I had forgotten how cold Gitche Gumee could be, even in the summer. I climbed to my feet, hoping to salvage what I could from the canoe. Fortunately, we had reached shallow water. Whitefoot waded to shore, while

Kanti and I gather what remained from the overturned canoe. I grabbed my fire starting kit as quickly as I could. I had wrapped it in an oiled deer skin. Hopefully, it hadn't gotten wet. We would need it to repair the canoe. I was sure the rock had damaged the left side.

Kanti grabbed the two moose skins. They were both soaked with water. I dragged the canoe toward shore. It had a small vertical tear on the left side. I found no other damage. We were lucky it wasn't worse.

There wasn't much of a beach. Only five paces of gravel separated the water from the birch trees at the edge of the woods. I found a forked stick and propped up one side of the canoe, making a small lean-to. It wasn't much, but it kept us out of the wind and rain. Whitefoot ignored the rain. He walked around, eager to check out his new surroundings. Nothing ever bothered him.

I could already see blue sky behind the rain clouds. The storm would end quickly. Not that it made much difference; the storm had done its damage. If I had been smart, I would have pulled into shore at the first sign of storm clouds. If I had, we would be safe on a sandy beach with an undamaged canoe.

"Chogan, we lost our food, and our moose skins are wet. You think we should turn back?" Kanti was cold and shivering. Wet hair clung to the back of her neck. I had seen drowned muskrats in better condition.

"If we can repair the canoe, I think we should continue," I said. "We'll find food along the way." I wished I was as optimistic as I sounded. We couldn't paddle a canoe for two days without food, and I was already hungry.

I was more optimistic about repairing the canoe. The gash in the side wasn't as large as I first thought, and I could find no other damage. If we could start a fire, it wouldn't take long to fix. The sun was already poking through the clouds and providing some warmth. The storm had hit hard and fast but was moving on. I unwrapped my spindle and hearth board; they were still dry.

"Kanti, see if you can find some dry wood. I'll gather some spruce pitch."

Normally, we gashed a spruce tree and then harvested the pitch the following year after it had time to accumulate. That wouldn't help now. Fortunately, spruce trees have natural injuries, often from deer or moose scratching their antlers against the tree to remove their velvet. We didn't need much pitch. The first six trees provided more than enough.

Kanti had firewood stacked by the canoe when I returned. Now all we needed was a fire. Fires are hard to start even in ideal conditions. The damp air would make it even more difficult. I placed a dry leaf under the notch in the hearth board. Then I inserted the cattail stem into the depression next to the notch and began to twirl. I pressed downward as I twirled the spindle. As my hands worked their way to the bottom, Kanti began spinning at the top. I watched the notch in the hearth board. A fine black dust should be filling the notch. I saw none. I feared our equipment was too damp. Finally, a small amount of tan dust began to fill the notch, but we needed black dust.

"We need to spin faster," I said.

The tan powder gradually turned black. I could smell it before I saw the smoke. Fine swirls of white smoke rose from under the spindle. We worked the spindle even harder, increasing our downward pressure as we spun the cattail. We didn't stop until smoke rose up from the dust in the hearth board notch. I gently blew on the smoking dust and it glowed red.

"Help me transfer the coals to the tinder bundle." I picked up the leaf under the coals and dropped it into the tinder bundle Kanti was holding. She wrapped the tinder bundle around the glowing coals and gently blew on it. The smoke increased and then the tinder bundle burst into flames. Kanti dropped it onto the ground next to the fire wood.

"Can you build up the fire while I cut a patch for the canoe?" I asked. Kanti nodded.

Making the patch was the easiest part of repairing the canoe. I chipped away at a stone until it had a sharp edge. Then I used the stone to cut a rectangular piece of bark from a birch tree.

Kanti had a good fire going when I returned. It made me wish we had food to cook. I placed the pitch on a flat stone and inserted it into the fire. It didn't take long for the pitch to soften. I transferred some of the softened pitch to the tear in the canoe with a stick. That alone should make the canoe water tight. To be on the safe side, I smeared pitch on the patch and pressed it against the tear.

"That should do it," I said.

The repair hadn't taken much time, and we were soon back on the water. If nothing else, it had given Whitefoot an opportunity to stretch his legs.

The storm had riled the water, and we now had rolling waves, but they were manageable. We continued paddling east along the shore of Gitche Gumee. Sandstone cliffs, some as high as thirty paces, replaced the gravel shoreline—we were lucky we beached when we did. Water seeping down from above stained the cliffs with a variety of colors. With a little imagination, one could see images imbedded in the cliffs.

The wind and water had eroded many sections of the cliffs, creating graceful arches. Some of the arches were so large we could paddle beneath them. We did so in silence. The view was so impressive; we didn't wish to diminish its beauty with words.

By late afternoon, we still hadn't found anything to eat. My stomach grumbled in protest. Whitefoot was also getting restless. He paced back and forth in the limited space the canoe provided.

If we didn't find food soon we would have to turn back. The cliffs along the shore gave way to sandy beaches. At least we could go to shore if the need were to arise.

"Kanti, see that river up ahead. Let's paddle up the river. Maybe we can find something to eat."

We hadn't gone far when the river widened into a large pond. Patches of *wapatoo* lined the shore. At least we wouldn't go hungry. I hadn't eaten *wapatoo* tubers since that spring day at Wagosh Lake.

Fire-Starting

Creating a fire was an important survival skill for individuals residing in northern climates. Most North American Indians used the more difficult two-piece hand drill method. This creates a fire by rubbing two materials together until they produced sufficient heat to ignite the powder created by the friction.

The two-piece set consists of a two or three foot spindle the diameter of the little finger and a half-inch thick hearth board. Chogan would carve an indentation the diameter of the spindle into the top of the hearth board about a spindle width from the edge. Then he must cut a 45 degree notch into the side of the hearth board with the point of the notch reaching the center of the indentation.

After inserting the spindle into the indentation, Chogan twirled the spindle between the palms of the hands. He gradually increase the twirling rate while pushing down on the spindle. His hands would work their way down the shaft of the spindle. When they reached the hearth board, Chogan returned his hands to the top of the spindle and continued spinning.

A fine powder collects in the notch as the spinning progresses. This will be light-colored at first, and then turn black as heat accumulates. Smoke will rise from under the spindle, but Chogan must continue twirling the spindle until the fine powder begins to smoke. This will occur when the temperature reaches about 800 degrees Fahrenheit. Once glowing embers are obtained, Chogan can add dry cattail fluff or other tinder while blowing on the embers until it bursts into flame.

The hand drill method is difficult at best, and not all woods and plant materials will work. Some of the better woods for the hearth board include cottonwood, redwood, yucca, and basswood. Often weeds such as cattail (Typha latifohia), common mullein (Verbascum thapsus), and horseweed (Conyza canadensis) make the best spindles.

Please see **The-gray-wolf.com/fire/**

"I think I hear lunch," Kanti said.

I assumed she was referring to the bullfrogs. From the sound, there had to be hundreds of them. Kanti grabbed her spear and stepped out of the canoe. Whitefoot jumped out to follow her, but I held him back. He would only scare the frogs.

"Whitefoot, you'll have to help me find *wapatoo* tubers." Apparently, he didn't find that suggestion exciting. He climbed up the riverbank and disappeared into the woods.

I loosened the *wapatoo* tubers with my bare feet, and as they floated to the surface, I threw them into the canoe. There were far more tubers than we could eat. I collected extra tubers to eat the following day. While I was gathering tubers, I discovered several crayfish lurking in the shallows. Crayfish aren't big, but they're tasty. I placed my left hand into the water in front of one of the crayfish to attract its attention while I grabbed it just behind the front pincers with my other hand. I threw it into the canoe with the *wapatoo* tubers. I gave up catching crayfish when I saw Kanti coming my way.

"Speared eight frogs," she said. She held up the frogs as proof. "I could have gotten more, but I was getting hungry."

"I got a bunch of *wapatoo* tubers and nine crayfish," I said. "Let's paddle back to the beach and eat what we have."

"Where's Whitefoot?" Kanti looked around. She had assumed Whitefoot was with me.

"He took off into the woods," I said. "He has a mind of his own. The beach isn't far from here. He'll sniff us out."

We climbed into the canoe and paddled back to the beach, paying particular attention to the crayfish at our feet. They were not happy about being plucked from the water, and we were afraid they might express their displeasure with their pincers. We pulled the canoe onto the beach with our toes still intact.

"Are you sure Whitefoot will find us?" Kanti asked.

"It's already late in the day, and we still have to eat. I think we've gone far enough. If he doesn't come back, he doesn't come back."

It had been an adventurous day and, despite our minor misfortune, quite enjoyable. Now the purpose of our trip was heavy on our hearts. Neither one of us wanted to leave Whitefoot. He was part of the family and our best defense against Ahanu and Taregan. We built a fire on the beach and roasted our *wapatoo* tubers, frog legs, and crayfish tails. It was an excellent meal, but we ate in silence. There was no sign of Whitefoot.

We laid our moose skins over the top of the canoe to catch what was left of the afternoon sun. With luck they would be dry by evening. The night would be cold, and we would need them. We had all but given up on Whitefoot when he came prancing up as if he were expecting to find us here. He immediately licked my eye sockets as was his custom. I don't know why he never did that to Kanti. I could smell dead animal on his breath, and he had dried blood in the hair around his mouth. He had found something to eat.

"Whitefoot, where have you been?"

I gave him a big hug as did Kanti. We gave Whitefoot a lot of attention that evening. I wondered if he understood the purpose of our trip. We felt like executioners. After giving him all that attention, tomorrow we would betray him and leave him on the beach. The thought of paddling away while he watched from the beach was more than I could bear. I considered disobeying Grandfather and returning to the village with Whitefoot, but I knew Grandfather was right. We had to leave Whitefoot. He was capable of taking care of himself, and he needed his freedom more than we needed a pet wolf.

As night fell, we wrapped ourselves in our moose skins and tried to sleep. The skins were sufficiently dry to provide warmth, and we had a stockpile of firewood to add the fire if we were to feel a chill. I wasn't looking forward to morning. Whitefoot lay between us, and we fell asleep stroking his fur.

I awoke with the morning sun shining in my eyes. It was one of the few times I awoke before Kanti. I reached over to pet Whitefoot, but he was gone. I added some wood to the remaining coals of the fire.

"Where's Whitefoot?" Kanti sat up and stretched.

"He was gone when I woke up," I said.

We ate the remaining *wapatoo* tubers—again in silence. We were hoping Whitefoot would show up, but we knew he was gone. I wondered if he had deserted us to spare us the pain of deserting him. We stalled as long as we could.

"Kanti, we need to be going," I said. Kanti nodded.

We loaded the canoe and pushed it into the river. We paddled out into the lake and headed west. Neither one of us looked back.

CHAPTER FOURTEEN

The Bear Returns

"Kanti, give it another push."

Kanti pushed the basket and stepped back, letting the basket swung freely from the tree limb. I closed my eyes and slowly pulled on the bow string. I visualized the arrow flying through the air, timing its flight. Only then did I release my arrow. It hit the target dead center. I wasn't as good as Grandfather. I couldn't hit the basket every time, but I was improving.

Fifteen days had passed since we abandoned Whitefoot, but it still fills me with guilt. Every night when I hear a wolf howl, I wonder if it is Whitefoot. And each morning, when I wake up, I reach down to stroke Whitefoot's fur, but he isn't there. I miss Whitefoot. Kanti hasn't said anything, but I am sure she feels the same way.

"Want me to give it another push?" Kanti asked.

"Give it a bigger push this time," I replied.

We should be checking our traps, but Mother had forbidden us to go. A large bear attacked five villages—six if you count the bear Whitefoot chased away. The bear hasn't killed anyone yet, although it injured people in several villages. The bear attacks at night, and only two people have actually seen the bear. Tonight representatives from all the villages would meet around our campfire and listen to the survivors' tales. Many people would gather around the campfire—too many for a boy of twelve winters to be invited. I would still listen from the shadows.

Kanti gave the basket a big push and stepped back. The basket was swinging faster than I had anticipated. I wanted a challenge, but not that great a challenge. I knew how long my arrow would take to reach the target. I visualized where the target would be when the arrow arrived. Then I released my arrow; it again hit the target. That was two out of two.

"Chogan, you are improving." It was Grandfather. He had a way of sneaking up when you least expected it.

"Thank you, Grandfather. I have been practicing."

"I assumed I would find you here."

"We should be checking our traps, but Mother forbids us to go. She is worried about the bear."

"This bear has many mothers worried," Grandfather said. "Tonight people will gather around the fire to decide the fate of this bear. There will be visitors from many villages."

"Yes, Grandfather, I have heard."

"We will need you at the gathering." Grandfather turned and left with no further comment.

"Why would they need you at the gathering?" Kanti asked.

"I don't know." Grandfather hadn't just given permission to attend the gathering; he said he *needed* me at the gathering. Surely, decisions would be made by the village elders, not boys of twelve winters.

I spent the afternoon snooping around the village. Everyone was talking about the bear. Opinions ranged from a mythical beast possessed by a demon to gross exaggerations of the misinformed. The bear sure looked real when I saw it. Hassun was of the opinion it was nothing more than a large bear and was willing to slay the bear should it cross his path.

By late afternoon, elders from the various villages began arriving. They wore garments artistically decorated with dyed porcupine quills and strings of multi-colored seeds, and their moccasins were made of the finest buckskin. Never before had I seen such beautiful clothes.

I wondered what a boy of twelve winters could do at a fire council of such importance. No other boy my age had been invited. I was feeling self-conscious, and the meeting had yet to begin. Perhaps Grandfather would change his mind once he saw the dignitaries from the neighboring villages.

Any hopes Grandfather would change his mind were dispelled when I returned to our wigwam. Grandfather was dressed in his finest clothes. He looked as impressive in his formal attire as did the elders from the other villages.

"Chogan, are you ready to go?" he asked.

"Yes, Grandfather." I wasn't sure that was the correct answer, but that was what Grandfather wanted to hear.

Most of the village elders had gathered around the fire before we arrived. I sat cross-legged next to Grandfather. Hassun arrived moments later and sat on my other side. That made me feel safer. At least I was sitting with friends.

One of our elders introduced the men from the other villages. This was followed by long-winded speeches. When they brought out the *opwaagan*, my palms began to sweat and fear twisted my stomach. Last time I smoked the *opwaagan* I almost threw up. It made me sick, just thinking about it. Hassun leaned toward me.

"You don't look so good," he said.

"I'm feeling sick," I replied.

"Don't inhale, Chogan. Just fill your cheeks and then exhale."

That was easier said than done. The *opwaagan* was rapidly moving in my direction. Each man took two puffs and passed it on. I took several deep breaths to calm my nerves—it didn't work. The *opwaagan* moved closer. I would vomit in front those village elders. Why had Grandfather insisted I come? Grandfather was now puffing on the *opwaagan*. I was next.

"Remember," Hassun whispered, "don't inhale."

Grandfather handed the *opwaagan* to me. I held it both hands as I had learned. I needed both hands just to keep it steady. I placed my lips around the stem and inhaled just enough to fill my checks as Hassun had recommended. Then I exhaled. That wasn't bad. As long as the smoke didn't reach my lungs, I was okay. I repeated it and then passed the *opwaagan* to Hassun. He took a deep breath and then exhaled a large smoke ring.

I had survived. The rest of the fire council should be easy. Now I could sit back and enjoy the stories. The *opwaagan* moved quickly around the circle. Finally, the leading elder stood to discuss the topic at hand.

"As you all know," he said. "We have gathered to discuss the bear attacks on our villages." The elder paused to allow this to sink in. I don't know why. We all knew why we were there. Personally,

I think he enjoyed standing in front of the group. That was something I would never do.

"This is no ordinary bear," he continued. "It is the size of five bears but has the power of ten bears. This bear has crushed wigwams under its weight, and it has injured many people. But do not believe me, my friends. Two men have seen this bear. We will now hear their tales." The elder sat down, and a man from a village to the west arose.

"This demon—for I shall not even call it a bear—attacked our village five days ago. It crushed two wigwams and destroyed much of our food. I saw this beast in the light of a quarter moon. It was large like a moose and had fire in its eyes. I shot an arrow at it, but it bounced off the large hump that grew between its shoulder blades. This animal is demon possessed. It is *Gitche Makwa* from the spirit world and cannot be killed." The man's words provoked a lively debate. Almost everyone had an opinion on the subject—all except Grandfather. Grandfather sat in silence.

Another man rose to his feet. "I too have seen this beast," he said. "Even in the darkness, I could see evil in the monster's eyes. Its claws were like fingers, and smoke belched from its nostrils. At the hump on the beast's shoulders, it was taller than a grown man. This creature is not of this earth. It must be from the spirit world." The man sat down. There was more discussion. Grandfather sat in silence.

Finally, Hassun rose to speak. "With due respect for the two brave men who have told their tales," Hassun said. "This is only a bear. A very large bear but still a bear. Darkness and fear have magnified its size until it is no longer real. No bear has claws as long as fingers. No bear is taller at its shoulders than a grown man. No bear has paws the size of lily pads." There were murmurs of disagreement, but Hassun continued. "We must hunt this bear like we hunt any bear. And then we must kill it." Hassun sat down.

His words were not well taken by those sitting at the circle, and the discussion became heated. People feared the consequences of provoking the spirit world. Some thought it best to allow the beast to have its way. Grandfather sat in silence. Words became harsh as discussion turned into arguments. I was afraid the arguments might extend beyond angry words. Then Grandfather rose to his feet. He stood there quietly until there was silence at the fire circle. Grandfather had a way of commanding respect. They waited for Grandfather to speak.

"We have heard tales from two men who have seen this animal in darkness," he said. "Let us now hear the tale from someone who has seen this animal in daylight."

I wasn't aware of a third person. The gossip before the meeting only mentioned two witnesses. Other people were also caught by surprise. There was much whispering. Hearing the tale from someone who had seen this creature in the daylight would add much to the discussion. I waited eagerly to hear his tale.

"Four moons ago my grandson, Chogan, encountered this bear while spearing fish on the river."

I couldn't believe what I was hearing. Grandfather was talking about me. That was why he wanted me at the fire council. He should have told me. Then I could have developed the most incurable illness to prevent my attendance.

"Chogan warned us of this bear. That brings great honor to Chogan. But we chose to ignore him, and that brings great shame to our village. It is time we listen to his tale."

Grandfather sat down and everyone looked toward me. I was a boy of twelve winters, and now Grandfather was expecting me to tell my tale to the elders of many villages. I crawled to my feet, but my knees were so weak I feared they might buckle. Given a choice, I would have preferred a good thrashing from Ahanu and Taregan.

"Last spring I was spearing fish along the river," I said. Every eye was upon me. No one talked or even whispered. "I speared this large trout." I spread my hands to show the length of the fish. I expected some laughter or crude remarks, but other than some nodding of heads, there was only silence. They were waiting for me to continue. "I carried the fish to shore and was about to add it to my stringer when I heard a crashing noise behind me. I assumed it was a bull moose plowing through the forest, but when I turned I discovered a great bear. The bear rose on its back legs and towered over me. I feared the bear would tear me apart with its long claws."

"How tall would you say the bear was when it stood on its back legs?" Grandfather asked.

I was trapped. Grandfather knew my answer. I couldn't change it now. If I told everybody, they would only laugh. There was no honorable way out of my predicament.

"It was as tall as two men," I said. "Maybe small men." I waited for the laughter, but the men in the circle only nodded.

"How long were the front claws?" Grandfather asked.

"As long as your fingers, Grandfather. And its paws were the size of lily pads."

"Was smoke belching from its nostrils?"

"No, Grandfather...but the bear did have bad breath." That brought a few snickers.

"Did you think it was anything other than a bear?"

"No, Grandfather. It was a bear, but it was a bear like no other bear I have ever seen."

"Thank you, Chogan. You have done well."

Grandfather stood up. I assumed that meant I was free to sit. I wasn't sure my knees could hold me much longer.

"As most of you know, many winters ago when I was in my youth, I journeyed west for several moons to the land with no trees."

I loved this story, although I didn't know what Grandfather's trip to the land with no trees had to do with the giant bear. It at least took attention away from me. I was thankful for that.

"I saw purple hills that rose up to kiss the sky," Grandfather said. "And the tops of the hills were covered with snow. Many strange animals lived at the base of these purple hills. I saw deer with antlers longer than my arm. There were other deer that were thick in the chest like a moose, but had large heads and shaggy fur. Sometimes these deer would cover the ground from horizon to horizon.

"While I was visiting the land with no trees, I saw another animal," Grandfather continued. "It was a great bear with claws as long as my fingers and paws the size of lily pads. When they stood on their rear legs, the larger bears were almost as tall as two men. Like the bear described in the tales we have heard tonight, they have a hump between the shoulder blades. What people have seen is not a beast possessed by the spirit world, but a bear that has journeyed to our forest from the land with no trees."

"How can we destroy such a bear," someone asked, "if arrows bounce off its skin?"

"Arrows have little effect on these animals. The arrows that do pierce their thick hide are no more than porcupine quills on a bobcat. They will only anger the bear."

"This beast might as well be possessed by demons if we cannot kill it," one of the elders said.

"They can be killed," Grandfather said. "My friends in the land with no trees showed me how it is done. It will require many men. One man cannot do it alone. They must use spears instead of arrows. And the spears must be attached to long poles so hunters can jab at the bear without coming within reach of its mighty claws. The bear's ribs are thick like lodge poles, and even hard driven spears cannot penetrate their chests. A brave hunter must work his way to the front of the bear while other hunters distract it with their spears. To kill this bear, a hunter must thrust his spear with all his might into its neck. If the spear hits the breathing tube or major blood vessels, the bear can be killed. That is the only vulnerable spot on this animal."

Hassun rose to his feet. "Then let us make spears with long shafts," he said. "Who will go with me to slay this bear?" Several men rose to their feet. There was much talking and shouting as the men whipped up their courage. I assumed the meeting was over. When no one was watching, I sneaked back to our wigwam.

CHAPTER FIFTEEN

The Rice Harvest

"Do you think Mother will let us gather rice today?" Kanti asked.

"I don't know," I said. "This bear scares Mother."

The bear was not a frivolous threat. It had attacked three more villages—all to the west of us. Hassun and the other hunters had searched the area but without success.

"If the bear comes after me, I'll stab him with my spear. Grandfather says a spear can kill the bear."

"Kanti, this bear is huge. It'll use your spear to pick its teeth—after it eats you!"

"Then I will give it indigestion."

I had no doubt she would. There were days when Kanti gave me indigestion. "We don't even know if you're going."

"You can't do it alone, and Grandfather can't help with his sprained ankle."

Wild rice grew in the shallow waters around our lakeshores and was a staple in our diet. When the rice became ripe in the fall, it had to be harvested quickly or the rice would fall into the water and be lost. If we were to have rice for winter, we would need to begin harvesting today.

We waited outside our wigwam for the verdict while Grandfather and Mother discussed the matter inside. Normally, Grandfather and I would have harvested the rice, but he had sprained his ankle on a recent hunt and couldn't kneel in a canoe for long periods. If we gathered rice, Kanti and I would have to do it.

Grandfather emerged from the wigwam with Mother. They both had heavy hearts. It had not been an easy decision. "Chogan," he said. "We'll need rice to see us through the winter. You and Kanti will have to harvest it for us."

"Yes, Grandfather. We will be happy to gather rice."

"This bear worries your mother, and rightly so, but you will be safe in your canoe. If you must come to shore, do so on one of the islands. There you will be safe."

That was all Kanti needed to hear. She immediately switched into her organizational mode. "I'll pack the food and baskets for the rice. Chogan, you fetch the paddles and moose robes." Kanti grabbed two baskets for storing the rice and then scurried off to organize her life—and mine. It would be a long two days.

The rice harvest was a major event in our village. For the next two days, canoes would cover the lake, and people would gather rice from dawn to dusk. It was a highly competitive event with the winners finding more food on their dinner table during the long winter.

It didn't take long to load the canoe. Despite Kanti's overbearing personality, she did have good organizational skills. She packed food for five days, even though we would be gone two days at most. After two days, the villagers would have the rice fields picked clean.

We pushed the canoe into the river and headed upstream toward the lake where Kanti had speared her bass. This time we would be after rice, not cattail reeds. I wished Whitefoot were with us, even though I knew we didn't have room for him. Our rice baskets occupied Whitefoot's space.

"I'm going to spear another bass," Kanti said.

"Yeah, and I'm going to shoot a flock of geese. We're after rice, Kanti, not fish. Remember?"

"But if I see a fish, I'm going to spear it."

"By the time you spear another bass, the rice will be gone," I said. To prove my point, I pointed to the other canoes racing up the river. "See the people in those canoes? They aren't after fish. They're after the same rice we are."

There were many canoes on the river, all heading toward the same lake. Unfortunately, Ahanu and Taregan were in one of the canoes. I backed off to maintain a safe distance. I was sure they would be too busy gathering rice to torment our lives, but there was no sense pressing our luck. They were still angry about the skunk and hornets, and we no longer had Whitefoot to protect us. When we entered the lake, they paddled toward the right, and I steered our canoe toward a rice patch on the opposite side of the lake.

"Do you know how to gather rice?" I asked.

"Of course I know how to gather rice."

"I'm only asking because you've never done this before." Kanti could get indignant over the smallest things.

"If you get the canoe to the rice, I'll get the rice into the canoe," Kanti said.

I paddled the canoe toward a nice patch of rice and waited for Kanti to hook the rice stalks with her curved stick. She pulled the stalks over the canoe, and then whacked the tips until grains of rice fell onto the deerskin at her feet. It was a simple procedure. I pushed my paddle against the lake bottom to move the canoe forward. As I did, Kanti pulled more rice stalks over the canoe. When she had collected a fair amount of rice on the deerskin, she transferred the grain to one of the two baskets. We had hopes of filling both baskets before we returned home the following evening.

One basket was half full when we stopped for a lunch of smoked fish and dried blueberries. For once I was glad Kanti packed plenty of food; I was starving. Gathering rice is not hard work, but it still made me hungry.

"Chogan, I think Ahanu and Taregan are heading this way." Kanti pointed toward the east.

I looked across the water in the direction Kanti was pointing. Ahanu and Taregan were definitely heading toward us, and it wasn't to pass the day. Kanti picked up her spear. I was hoping the spear wouldn't be needed. There was little Ahanu and Taregan could do to us from their canoe, unless they wanted to get wet.

"Hey, Bearslayer. You're in our rice patch."

"The lake belongs to our village. We have as much right here as you do," I told Ahanu.

"Ahanu, I think the rice in their basket must belong to us," Taregan said.

"But we shouldn't take all their rice," Ahanu replied. "That would be greedy." Ahanu turned to me. "Chogan, we'll let you keep half of it, but that's only because we're nice guys."

"You aren't getting any of our rice," I said.

"Who's to stop us?" Ahanu asked. "You don't have that wolf to protect you anymore."

"Ahanu, why don't we return at the end of the day?" Taregan said. "Then we can take all of their rice. That way they won't owe us anything for tomorrow."

"We'll see you tonight, Chogan." Ahanu and Taregan pushed off with their paddles and headed for another rice patch.

"Do you think they'll come back?" Kanti asked.

"They will if they think they can get something for nothing."

We finished our lunch and went back to work, but no matter where we went on the lake, Ahanu and Taregan were never out of sight. We continued filling our baskets with rice. We would have to deal with Ahanu and Taregan when the time came.

"Chogan, there's a snake!" There are few things in life that scare Kanti. Water snakes was one of them.

"That's just a water snake. It isn't poisonous."

"I don't care. Let's get out of here."

"The snakes are all over the lake," I told her. "They have sharp teeth and a nasty disposition, but if you leave them alone they won't bite you."

Kanti wasn't convinced, so I paddle toward another rice patch. Today there were plenty of patches to choose from. Tomorrow most of them would be picked clean, all the more reason for working hard today. By late evening, we had one of the baskets filled to the brim.

"Where are we going to spend the night?" Kanti asked. "Grandfather wanted us to sleep on one of the islands."

"There are plenty of islands to choose from. How about that island?" I pointed to a small island covered with stunted birch trees and bushy shrubs.

"Chogan, it's covered with poison ivy. We can't sleep there."

"I think it's perfect," I said. "Do you think we could store all our rice in the deerskin?"

"If we wrapped it tightly, I think it'll all fit," Kanti replied. "What do you have in mind?"

"See that mud next to the shore?" I said. "We need to smear that on our arms and legs." Ahanu and Taregan watched us with interest, but they were too far away to understand what we were doing.

We covered our arms and legs with mud to protect us from the poison ivy. Then, to be on the safe side, we used lily pads between our hands and the poison ivy vines when we cleared the open area where we expected to sleep. With the surrounding brush providing cover, Ahanu and Taregan couldn't see us pour our rice onto the deer skin.

"We still have some daylight. Let's refill the baskets."

"With what?" Kanti asked.

"Water snakes," I said.

"Yuck!"

"Kanti, you can paddle the canoe. I'll catch the snakes."

We paddled around the shallows where the snakes liked to hide. It didn't take long to find one.

I grabbed it behind the head. It opened its mouth and hissed. A row of sharp teeth lined its mouth. I wouldn't want to get bitten by a water snake even if they weren't poisonous. It had to be painful. I placed the snake into the basket and replaced the cover. By the time it was dusk, we had collected fifteen snakes. We returned to our island and divided the snakes between the two baskets.

"What if they come up the path from the canoe?" Kanti asked.

"We'll build our fire on the path, but unless my guess is wrong, they'll sneak through the bushes. They prefer to be sneaky."

Manoomin

Manoomin, also known as wild rice, was a dietary staple for Native Americans throughout the western Great Lakes region. As long as it was kept dry, the wild rice stored well during the cold winter months when other plant foods were unavailable. Manoomin was so vital to the survival of the Ojibway Indians that it was not uncommon for wars to be fought over the ownership of the more productive rice fields.

Manoomin is a tall grass (up to ten feet) that thrives in the shallow waters of lakes and slow flowing streams throughout the Midwest. The leaves are long and slender and can grow to a length of three feet. At maturity the broom-like flower clusters at the tips of the plants evolve into three-quarter-inch, black seeds (rice). Stiff husks encase the seeds until the seeds are expelled into the water to produce more manoomin the following year.

Indians harvested manoomin in the fall, just before the seeds separated from the husks. A man in the rear of a canoe pushed it among the tall grass with a long pole while the woman in the front of the canoe gathered the manoomin stalks with a curved stick, forcing the rice-bearing tops over the front of the canoe. Then she would beat them with another stick until the rice fell onto deer hide where it was collected.

After harvesting, women parched the rice over a slow fire to loosen the husks. Once the husks were loosened, they poured the grain into deerskin-lined pits and trampled it with their feet to separate the rice from the husks. Finally, the rice and husks were tossed up and down on a birch bark tray, which allowed the wind to blow away the husks.

Please see **The-gray-wolf.com/manoomin/**

We spread our moose skins on the ground to protect us from any remaining poison ivy. Then we lay on our moose skins; although neither of us could sleep. It wasn't long before we heard splashing from a canoe slicing through the water. For people trying to be sneaky, Ahanu and Taregan made a lot of noise. They couldn't sneak up on a dead turtle. They beached their canoe and began crawling in from the east. Not only were there poison ivy vines on that side, there were also wild raspberry bushes with sharp thorns. Ahanu and Taregan had just discovered the thorns. I could hear them cussing.

Despite the thorns, they continued and were almost to the clearing. Even though I had my eyes mostly closed, I could see their hands reaching out from the brush to grab our baskets. I hoped they liked snakes.

They must have been proud of their accomplishment, as they were even noisier on their way back to their canoe and no longer bothered to whisper. We could hear them clearly.

"We got both baskets," Ahanu said. "Let's get out of here…"

"Easy, Ahanu. You're tipping the canoe…"

"No I'm not. How full are the baskets?" Ahanu asked.

"How would I know?" Taregan replied. "It's too dark to see into the baskets."

"Reach into the basket with your hand, Stupid. Must I tell you everything?"

"Ouch! A snake bit me. The basket's filled with snakes."

"You idiot, you knocked over the basket. Now the snakes are all over the canoe."

"Ouch!"

I heard two splashes: Ahanu and Taregan had decided to go for a swim. "I think that will keep Ahanu and Taregan busy for the rest of the night," I told Kanti. She just snickered. We heard more splashing. Then there was silence. "Ahanu and Taregan must have gone off to lick their wounds," I said.

I say there was silence, but there is never silence in the wild. The croaking of frogs was persistent, and occasionally, we could hear an owl hoot. I was almost asleep when I heard a wolf howl. It was off in the distance.

"Do you think that was Whitefoot?" Kanti asked.

"I don't know," I said. "I like to think it was."

"Will we ever see him again?"

"Wolves are private creatures," I said. "We will be lucky if we ever see another wolf."

We lay there in silence, deep in our own thoughts. Finally, we fell asleep. When we awoke the sun was shining. We quickly ate our breakfast and packed the moose skins into the canoe. Several canoes were already on the lake. We found our rice baskets along the shoreline where Ahanu and Taregan had dumped them. One basket still contained a snake. I thanked the snake and released it unharmed. Then we refilled the baskets with our rice and headed out on the lake. Most of the rice patches were now picked clean, but by late afternoon we had found enough rice to fill our baskets.

"You ready to head back?" I knew I was. My legs were stiff from the constant kneeling in the canoe.

"If we hurry, we can be back in time for supper," Kanti said.

Kanti was always thinking of food. I steered the canoe toward the river opening, and we were soon sucked into the river's current. Our arms were sore and our backs were aching by the time we arrived at our village, but it felt good to stand up and stretch our legs. I pulled the canoe onto the shore and grabbed a basket of rice. Kanti grabbed the other basket.

"We're back," I told Mother when we arrived at our wigwam. "We filled both baskets."

"You did well," Mother said after inspecting the baskets. "Did you have any problems?"

"No, Mother."

"You're lucky. A couple of boys were bitten by water snakes. They said the snakes crawled right into their canoe. I've never heard of such a thing."

"Those snakes can be mean," I said.

"They also slept on some poison Ivy. I saw one of the boys, and he was covered with weeping sores."

"Maybe you should give him some of your fish oil," I said. "I'm sure he deserves it."

CHAPTER SIXTEEN

The Magic Arrow

"Kanti, if you're coming with me, you'd better hurry." It's easier to motivate a dead toad than to prod Kanti into action when she's talking to a girlfriend. I headed down the trail without her. I hadn't gone far when she came running after me with spear in hand.

"Wait for me, Chogan."

I continued walking, letting Kanti run until she caught up. After ten days Mother was finally letting us check our traps, and I wanted to make good my escape before she changed her mind. All the bear encounters had been west of our village, and none were within the last eight days. Grandfather said the bear probably returned to the land with no trees. That logic failed to convince

Mother. If our traps hadn't been on the east side of our village, she never would have given in.

"Chogan, if we caught a rabbit ten days ago, will the rabbit still be in the snare?"

"No, but the coyotes and fox would be well fed."

Kanti did bring up a valid point: Most of our traps will have been sprung. If we caught anything, the fruits of our labor would be dead and rotting or eaten by predators. The first three traps confirmed my suspicions. All three traps were sprung without evidence of having caught anything. By the time we approached our last three traps at the north end of Wagosh Lake, all we had was a rabbit. Our next trap was a deadfall on a beaver trail. I had propped up the end of a heavy log. If the trap worked as planned, the log would fall on a beaver. Even from a distance I could see it was tripped. I was hoping for a fresh beaver to add to our take.

"Yuck!" Kanti said as we approached the trap.

That summed up my feelings. The log had clobbered a beaver, but some animal had pushed the log aside and devoured our catch. All that remained were the tail and some intestines.

"Bear," I said. I didn't have to tell Kanti which one. The paw prints in the mud were the size of lily pads.

"Should we turn back?" Kanti asked.

That was the logical choice. I gave it some thought, but we only had two traps left, and they were nearby. I also needed to get Mother's blue basket from the climbing tree. We had never retrieved it, and now Mother was looking for it.

"These tracks are old. The bear was here yesterday," I said. "Let's check the next two traps, get Mother's blue basket out of the climbing tree, and then head for home."

Even though the bear could have traveled a great distance in a day, I wasted no time checking the remaining traps. Neither trap was sprung. I left them as they were and headed toward the climbing tree. It wouldn't take long to retrieve the basket. I scanned the shoreline as we approached. Animals congregated around rivers and lakes when thirsty. I didn't wish to surprise any animal bigger than myself. I saw nothing other than a water snake and several frogs. They didn't scare me. What scared me were the fresh bear tracks in the mud. Kanti didn't notice the tracks, and I didn't point them out. I didn't want her to worry. At the moment, she was more concerned with something across the lake.

"Look, Chogan, a wolf."

Kanti pointed to the east shore of the lake. It was a long way off, but I could see an animal the size of a wolf drinking from the lake.

"Do you think that could be Whitefoot?" Kanti asked.

"If it is, he's found a friend." Another wolf had joined the first. "I doubt if Whitefoot could have traveled this far. He's still far to the east of us. But we need to grab the basket and get out of here."

"I'll get the basket."

Kanti ran for the climbing tree and quickly scampered to the top where the basket was tied. She then began working her way down the tree with one hand on the basket and the other hand on a branch. I turned my back to study the bear tracks in the mud. Some of the tracks were at the water's edge where small ripples of water were slowly eroding them. As I watched, one of the tracks disappeared entirely. The bear had made those tracks moments before we arrived.

"Kanti, forget the basket. We need to go...Now!"

"I'm almost down."

My body quivered when I heard a limb snap followed by a thud. I knew what had happened before I turned around. Kanti was lying on the ground, grimacing with pain. Her left leg was bent where legs don't naturally bend.

"Where are you hurt?" I asked.

"Just my leg. I twisted my leg when I fell."

"You broke your leg," I said. "We'll need to splint it." I had seen Grandfather splint a leg, but I had never done it myself. "Wait here. I'll get some birch bark."

There were many birch trees along the lake. I found one with a clear patch of bark and cut out a rectangular section with the sharp edge of my magic arrowhead. I could use the cord from one of my snares to bind the splint. Finally, I gathered cattail fluff to use as padding. When I returned to the climbing tree, Kanti was still grimacing in pain. She would not like what I had to do next.

"Kanti, I need to straighten your leg before I apply the splint. It'll hurt."

"It can't hurt more than it does now," she said. "Do what you must do. Just do it quickly."

"Grandfather says it helps to bite on something. Try biting on the shaft of your spear."

Kanti placed the spear in her mouth, and I pulled on her leg. That had to hurt. Kanti had tears in her eyes, but never cried out in pain. I pulled harder, and the leg became straight.

"I'm sorry, Kanti. I had to do that." Kanti nodded. I think I had as many tears in my eyes as she did. "That's the worst part. Now I'm going to splint the leg to make sure it stays straight."

I lined the birch bark with the cattail fluff and slipped it under her leg. Then I bound it together with the cord from my snare. It wasn't pretty, but it kept the leg straight.

"What will we do now?" Kanti asked. "I can't walk and I'm too heavy for you to carry. You'll have to leave me here and go for help."

"I'm not leaving you," I said. "It'll be dark soon. We'll spend the night here and wait for help to arrive in the morning."

"How will they find us?"

"I'll build a fire," I said. "Then I'll add some wet leaves. They'll see the smoke."

"Can't we make the smoke now?" Kanti asked.

"They won't miss us until dark, and then they won't see the smoke. We'll still need a fire. The night will be cold, and we don't have blankets."

I didn't tell Kanti the real reason for the fire. Grandfather says bears don't like fire. If this was where the bear comes to drink, he could return. I looked around for a better spot. It had to be close; I couldn't carry Kanti very far. The best spot would be at the base of a rock wall not far from where I stood.

"Kanti, grab around my neck." I picked Kanti up and carried her to the rock wall, where I tried to make her comfortable. But I had little time. It would soon be dark, and I needed firewood. I found an oak that had blown down the previous winter. The wood should be dry. I broke off as many branches as I could. If we kept the fire small, the wood should last until morning.

I built two small fires in front of us like Grandfather had taught me. One large fire would make the front of us too hot while our backs remained cold. If we sat between the rock wall and two fires, heat would bounce off the wall and warm our backs. I hoped I had gathered enough wood to last the night.

Night fell quickly and the woods closed in upon us. Everything beyond the fire was darkness. I hoped Grandfather was right about bears hating fire. If a bear were to charge out of the darkness, it would be upon us before we could react. Just the same, I kept my bow and quiver at my side. Kanti slept fitfully as her pain permitted. Even as she slept, her right hand clutched her spear. From what Grandfather said, Kanti's short spear and my arrows would only irritate the bear.

I added more wood to the fire. I was exhausted and would have enjoyed some sleep, but I had to remain awake to keep the fire burning. Several times during the night, I heard deep growls and rustling in the bushes. I knew the bear was watching us. So far the fire was working. As long as we had firewood, we were safe.

Half way through the night, I heard snorting off to my right. I looked into the darkness and saw the bear illuminated in the firelight. It was bigger than I remembered. We were low on firewood, but I added a log to one of the fires anyway. The bear backed away. After hearing no further noise, I sat down and began to relax.

***

"Wake up, Chogan!"

I felt the blunt end of Kanti's spear poking me in the ribs. It took a moment to realize where I was. Then I woke up in a hurry. The sun was peeking through the trees in the east, and one fire had burned out. How could I have been so careless as to fall asleep? We were lucky to be alive. I added more wood to the remaining fire.

"How are you feeling this morning?" I asked.

"Better. I think the splint helps. I heard the bear last night. It came after us, didn't it?"

"If it did, it's gone now," I said. I didn't need to explain that we would be dead if it had stayed around. The fire, now blazing, made me feel more secure. With the increased visibility daylight provided, I found courage to search for more firewood. I didn't find as much wood as I would have liked, but we had enough to make it through the morning.

"Do you think Grandfather will be looking for us?" Kanti asked.

"Grandfather, Hassun, and half the village will be looking for us," I said. "They would have left at first light."

"Shouldn't we put some wet leaves on the fire to make smoke?"

"How much pain are you having?" I asked.

"Not too bad," She said. "What does that have to do with making smoke?"

I knew she was lying. Her facial muscles were tense and her eyes were watery. She was fighting back tears. What I was about to suggest would only make her pain worse.

"If I carried you to the climbing tree, do you think you could climb it with two arms and one leg?"

"Why would we want to do that?" she asked. "The fire is keeping the bear away."

"But no one can see the fire. If I add wet leaves to make smoke, the fire will lose its heat. Smoke won't keep away a bear—not this bear."

Kanti didn't hesitate in answering. The logic of what I was saying was obvious. We had no other choice.

"If you can get me to the tree, I'll climb to the highest branch if needed." Kanti forced herself to a sitting position. "Can I take my spear with me?"

"If you can climb the tree, I'll bring your spear up to you."

I added wet leaves to the fire, and a column of white smoke rose into the sky. As I had expected, the fire now gave off little heat—not enough to discourage a bear.

"Are you ready?" I asked.

Kanti grabbed her spear with one hand and placed her other arm around my neck. I lifted her up as gently as I could. Even though she wasn't heavy, I was glad the climbing tree wasn't far away. The area if front of us was open with few trees and bushes, although the ground was uneven and covered with rocks, making the walk difficult. I tried to walk carefully, but Kanti still grimaced with each step. We were half way to the climbing tree when I heard a thrashing noise coming from a small ravine. I was hoping for a moose, but when I heard the deep roar, I knew I was not that lucky. The enormous bear pushed its massive body through the brush and stepped into the clearing. It growled again, this time deeper and more prolonged, making the woods around me shutter. I turned and ran for our fire even though I knew I couldn't outrun the bear. I hadn't gone far when my foot slipped on the rocks, and we fell to the ground. Kanti's muscles tighten and she cried out with pain. Then she raised her spear toward the bear. It was a hopeless gesture. Her small spear was as useless as my arrows. Grandfather said arrows would only irritate the bear like porcupine quills on a bobcat, not that it mattered. I had left my bow and quiver by the fire.

The bear charged toward us, growling as it came. When it was two paces from us, it rose up on its hind legs, as it had done on the riverbank. The bear stood as high as two men. Its claws were as long as fingers, and its paws were the size of lily pads. This time I had no fish to distract it. The bear was preparing to crash down on us with its full weight, and there was nothing I could do to prevent it. I pulled Kanti to my side. If we were to die, we would die together. Kanti held up her spear, but the bear pushed it aside with its paw. This was the end. I would never see another winter.

Then I felt a gust of air brush against my cheek as a blur of gray fur leaped over my shoulder. Whitefoot landed just in front of us with fangs bared. His deep-throated snarls even filled me with fear. He immediately nipped at the bear's hind leg, drawing blood. The bear, now filled with rage, twisted to swat at Whitefoot with its huge paw, but Whitefoot was no longer there. He was now biting at the bear's other foot. Whitefoot remained one step ahead of the bear as they spun in circles.

Whenever the bear stopped, Whitefoot bit into its rear legs. I knew Whitefoot was pressing his luck. Sooner or later, the bear would anticipate Whitefoot's move, and Whitefoot would suffer the same fate as his mother. Then Kanti and I would be next.

I couldn't help Kanti while sitting on the ground where I was. I jumped to my feet and ran for my bow and quiver. Even if my arrows only aggravated the bear, they might distract it. Perhaps I could get the bear to chase me. Then I could lead it away from Kanti.

I grabbed my bow and reached into my quiver for an arrow, but not any arrow. I searched the quiver until I found the arrow with the enchanted arrowhead. If any arrow could pierce the bear's thick hide, it would be the magic arrow. I notched the arrow on the bow string and waited. I couldn't shoot while Whitefoot and the bear were spinning around. I might hit Whitefoot. I waited. After a moment, the bear caught Whitefoot with its massive paw and sent him flying through the air. Whitefoot landed on the ground next to Kanti and lay still. I hoped he only had the wind knocked out of him.

I was now free to shoot the bear, but I couldn't see its throat. Grandfather said that was the bear's only weakness. I waited. With the wolf no longer a threat, the bear charged toward Kanti. I knew the bear would stop in front of her and rise up on its hind legs. I had seen the bear do it twice before. It would then come down on Kanti with all its weight. I closed my eyes and pulled back on the bowstring. I mentally watched the arrow fly through the air toward the bear, timing the arrow as it flew—just as Grandfather had taught me. Then I open my eyes and aimed above the bear's head. I aimed at a spot as high as two men. I waited. Timing had to be perfect. If I released the arrow too soon, it would fly harmlessly over the bear's head. I would never get a second chance. I waited. When the bear's front paws left the ground, I released the arrow. It flew true. As I expected, the bear rose to its full height and spread its front paws as it prepared to plunge down on my sister. It was now as tall as two men. It was just about to crash down on Kanti when the magic arrow slammed into its throat. The bear shook its head angrily, trying to dislodge the arrow. Then the bear looked in my direction and opened his massive jaws. A gurgling snarl that was filled with pure meanness gushed forth from its throat.

The bear would have come down on top of Kanti if she hadn't rolled out of the way. The angry beast snarled again and swatted at the arrow protruding from its neck. It broke the shaft of the arrow, but the arrowhead remained deeply lodged in its neck. It spun around two more times. Kanti stabbed her spear into its belly. The bear roared once more and then ran into the woods and was gone. The woods was strangely silent. I didn't know if the bear would come back. If it did, there was nothing more we could do. As I ran to Kanti, Whitefoot rose to his feet. He didn't appear severely injured. He trotted off to the north as if nothing had happened. I hadn't seen her before, but a she-wolf was waiting for him on a small knoll not far from us. I was sure she was bewildered by Whitefoot's behavior. Whitefoot was half way to the knoll when he turned to look back at us, as if he were trying to make up his mind. It was a difficult decision. After a brief hesitation, he ran to the she-wolf. Grandfather was right. Whitefoot was a wild animal. He had made the right choice. He belonged in the woods with his own kind, but we would still miss him.

I carried Kanti back to the fire. Neither one of us had any fight left. If the bear returned it would be over for us. I made Kanti as comfortable as I could and then added more wet leaves to the fire. The sun was high in the sky, and we were both asleep when Grandfather and Hassun found us. Hassun blew on a wooden whistle, and more hunters arrived.

"Are you okay?" Grandfather asked. We both nodded.

Grandfather made a stretcher from two poles and netting woven with cord from my snares while Hassun and several other hunters went after the bear. Perhaps with some luck, they would find the bear and kill it. I hoped so. I did not want to ever run into the bear again. The rest of the men took turns carrying Kanti on the stretcher. It was almost dark when we reached the village. Everyone wanted hear the details of our adventure, but I hadn't slept much during the night and was too exhausted to talk. Mother gave me something to eat and then I crawled onto my sleeping bench and fell asleep.

When I awoke the following morning, the sun was streaming through the hole in the top of the wigwam. It took a moment to realize what had happened was not a dream. I looked over at Kanti's sleeping bench: It was empty. She couldn't be in too much pain. I could hear her outside the wigwam telling her friends about the huge bear she had speared. There would be no living with her now. Grandfather and Hassun were also talking, but I couldn't hear what they were saying. Then they entered the wigwam.

"You are awake," Grandfather said. "The sun is high in the sky. You slept through the night and most of the day."

"I could sleep another day," I said. "Is Kanti going to be okay?"

"It will be several moons before she can use her leg, but she will walk again," Grandfather said. "You made an excellent splint."

"You have brought great honor to your family," Hassun said.

"Were you able to track the bear?" I asked. "Someone needs to kill that bear before it hurts someone else."

Hassun looked at Grandfather in bewilderment. "Your grandfather didn't tell you?" he asked.

It was my turn to be confused. "I just woke up," I said. "I haven't talked to Grandfather since we arrived in the village last night."

"We tracked the bear, but we didn't track it far. We found it no more than two hundred paces from where we found you. The arrow you shot severed several blood vessels in its neck. It almost went through the neck. Where did you find such an arrowhead? I have never seen anything like it," Hassun said.

"I found it in a cave."

"The shaft was broken, but we saved the arrowhead." Hassun handed me the mystic arrowhead, now stained with blood. I would have to make another shaft for it, although I hoped I would never need it again. A magic arrowhead must be used wisely. With luck such a need would only happen once in a lifetime. But who knows what the future will bring. A lot had happened since I first encountered the bear along the riverbank. It had tried to kill me twice. Even so, I felt no hatred for the bear. The bear was a hunter like me, but sometimes the hunter becomes the hunted. I have been both the hunter and the hunted. Luck and perhaps some skill had been on my side, and I had survived.

There were no further bear attacks, and life returned to normal in our village. Leaves fell from the trees, and snow again covered the ground.

Kanti and I continued checking our snares and deadfalls, but it was more difficult in the deep snow.

Now and then, when the moon was high, I would hear a wolf howl and I would wonder if it was Whitefoot. At other times, I would find tracks in the snow, and I liked to think they belonged to Whitefoot. He saved my life, and I needed to thank him. Someday I hope to see him again. Until then, I will treasure my memories of Whitefoot, and I will sing his praises around the council fires. I will tell all who will listen of that day at Wagosh Lake, when Whitefoot turned back one last time to look at me as if to say, "We're even now, my friend."

SUPPORT INDIE AUTHORS

If you enjoyed this novel, please consider leaving some stars on Amazon.com. You don't need to write a comment, although that is also acceptable. The choice of stars can be found at https://www.amazon.com/dp/ 0989247708

Web pages from Chogan and the Gray Wolf

Some of you may have missed Chogan's web pages while reading the book. If so, below are some of the web pages that accompany the novel. Copy the underlined section into your computer's search engine to view the web page.

The-Gray-Wolf.com/baggataway This web page describes the Indian game of baggataway, which we now call lacrosse. There are also pictures of Fort Michilimackinac where a game of baggataway turned into a massacre during the Pontiac rebellion.

The-Gray-Wolf.com/snares This web page shows how Chogan made the snares he uses to catch small game.

The-Gray-Wolf.com/wapatoo Wapatoo (also known as arrowhead) is an edible plant. This web page shows how to identify the plant and cook the tubers.

The-Gray-Wolf.com/copper Thousands of years ago an ancient race of people mined copper in Michigan's Upper Peninsula. This web page shows the types of copper they mined and well as a typical mine.

The-Gray-Wolf.com/cord This web page shows how to make string and rope out of milkweed fiber.

The-Gray-Wolf.com/fire Need to start a fire without matches? This web site will show you how Chogan starts a fire with a spindle and fireboard.

The-Gray-Wolf.com/manoomin Find out how Chogan and harvested their wild rice.

If you liked *Chogan and the Gray Wolf,* you will probably enjoy book #2 in the Chogan Native American Series.

Chogan and the White Feather

Life along the southern shore of Lake Superior would be pleasant, if not for the village bully, and every Indian village had one. Unfortunately, twelve-year-old Chogan and his ten-year-old sister Kanti have the misfortune of residing in a village with two bullies. But size isn't everything, and Chogan and Kanti's devious tactics usually gets the best of Ahanu and Taragan. That all changes hen Kanti unwittingly bets her prized spear against Ahanu's bear-claw necklace. If Kanti is to win the wager and reclaim her spear, she will need the assistance of Mishosha (the Magician of the Lake) and Gitche Migizi (an eagle so large men can ride on its back).

Life becomes even more difficult when Chogan and Kanti come face-to-face with the Windigo—a stretch of river so treacherous villagers named it after a mythical beast that devours human flesh. During a full moon the wailing of a thousand souls can be heard within Windigo's mournful roar. If Chogan and Kanti are not careful, their voices will be added to that number.

ABOUT THE AUTHOR

About the author:

Larry Buege is a retired physician assistant who lives with his wife along the southern shore of Lake Superior. His literary work has won both regional and international awards. He writes in a variety of genres although his Chogan Native American Series is most popular. The Native American Series follows an Ojibway family in the year 100 B.C. (Before Columbus). In addition to the short stories and novels, the author has been a frequent contributor to Primative Technology magazine.

The Native American series is unique in that each novel has references to six to eight stand-alone websites with color photos that demonstrate skills Chogan must learn to survive in the virgin forest.

Larry Buege

Made in the USA
Las Vegas, NV
07 December 2024

7f78f5e9-d6b1-41b6-9f79-26414633a877R01